He's more than a man—he's a fabulous father!

Dear Reader,

One of the reasons I enjoyed writing *First Time, Forever* so much is that the hero is younger than the heroine. The age difference between Evan and Kathleen is seven years, which, coincidentally, is the age difference between my real-life hero and me! What our incredible time together has taught me is that when you say yes to the song of your heart—never mind all those rules—it keeps you forever young. Oh, the hair still has silver threads in it, and the wrinkles appear, but the feeling in your heart of being alive—on fire—gets stronger, rather than diminishing.

When I wrote *First Time, Forever* I wanted it to be a book that honors the fire in each of us, while at the same time honoring our longing for the traditions that have carried us safely this far—marriage and family.

My greatest hope is that this book will bring you to a place of laughter and tenderness, tears and triumph.

With my sincerest best wishes,

Cara Colter

Fabulous
FATHERS

CARA COLTER
First Time, Forever

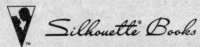

Silhouette® Books

Published by Silhouette Books
America's Publisher of Contemporary Romance

SILHOUETTE BOOKS

PLEASE RECYCLE
THIS PRODUCT IS RECYCLABLE

ISBN-13: 978-0-373-18892-5

FIRST TIME, FOREVER

Recycling programs
for this product may
not exist in your area.

CARA COLTER

lives on an acreage in British Columbia with her partner, Rob, and eleven horses. The mother of three grown children and a grandmother of one, she is a recent recipient of a *Romantic Times BOOKreviews* Career Achievement Award in the Love and Laughter category. Cara loves to hear from readers. You can contact her, or learn more about her, through her Web site at www.cara-colter.com.

To Richard, who makes my life so much
"richer" in every way.

Chapter One

Evan Atkins had the book hidden behind a copy of *Sports Illustrated*. He drank his coffee and frowned at the words, trying to concentrate, but finding it difficult with all the commotion at the Hopkins Gulch Café this morning.

The café had six tables, two booths and a lunch counter. There were coffee cups half filled, and bacon and eggs half eaten at nearly all those tables, but the seats, save for the one Evan inhabited at a booth, were empty, abandoned.

The guys were three deep at the window, trying to get a look at the Outpost, the town's general store, across the street. A strange car was parked out front, a U-haul trailer behind it. The car had caused this great stirring of interest when a pair of strangers had emerged from it. Both of them had looked around briefly, and then disappeared into the Outpost.

"If they were just askin' for directions," Sookie Peters said wisely, "they would have left the engine running."

"Did you see her?" Jack Marty asked for about the sixtieth annoying time. "She looked just like Julia Roberts. I swear. Well, maybe a little older. And not scrawny like Julia." He said this with easy familiarity, as if Julia were his second cousin.

"Nah, she dint," Sookie said. "More like the other one. The one from the movie about the bus. That's who she looked like."

"Sandra Bullock?" Cal, Sookie's brother, hooted. "She did not!"

"Oh, what do you know?"

The banter went back and forth, Evan furrowing his brow and trying to ignore the nonsense as best he could. All those guys at the window should take a lesson from him. Good things did not necessarily come in pretty packages.

Millie came and refilled his coffee cup. He didn't quite get the *Sports Illustrated* up fast enough or high enough, and she caught sight of the book hidden behind it, crooked her head, read the title, and smiled.

If she told the guys he was never going to live it down.

Potty-Training for the Hopelessly Confused.

But she just smiled, in that way he was never going to get used to, as if being a single dad made him adorable to the female populace, like a teddy bear.

"Where is Jesse this morning?" she asked.

"I dropped him off at Beth's Day Care for a while."

"That's good. He needs to be with other kids sometimes."

"So I've been told." Evan scowled at the book. Step Five: Pray.

He thought that was a mighty strange step to include in a book on potty-training, not scientific at all. On the other hand, when his son had gone missing and he had done everything he knew how to do, applied all his intellect and strength and devotion, *everything,* to getting Jesse back, and nothing had worked, isn't that what his days had become?

Please God, please God, please God. If You can't bring my baby home, look after him. It would shock those guys at the window to know he had done that, prayed every day, but he'd been shocked himself the first time those words had gone through his head. Shocked, and then surprised, the words bringing him the only measure of peace he'd had in those desperate years.

Jesse was home now. Okay, it had taken two years, but then Evan would admit to being somewhat rusty in the prayer department, since he'd spent most of his youth moving in the other direction, hell bound.

Still, a two-year wait was a might scary thought in terms of potty-training.

It was very hard to formulate a proper potty-training prayer with all the commotion at the window.

"What do you suppose she's doing over there?"

Millie, known for her foghorn voice, called out, "You know Pa hasn't been feeling so hot. They tried to sell the place, but now they're just hoping to get someone to run it for them."

"That would mean she'd have to live here," Mike Best pointed out sagely.

The crowd at the window contemplated that for a few minutes of blessed silence that allowed Evan to review his prayer. He decided to keep it simple. *God, help.* Satisfied, he looked back at the book.

And realized he had read it incorrectly.

It didn't say *pray.* Step Five said *play.*

He read carefully: *Be sure and make potty-training fun. A game.*

The guys at the window started up again, sounding like a gaggle of old hens excited about an unexpected windfall of worms.

"Hey, there's the kid. He's coming out by hisself, though."

"Don't he look like trouble?"

"Aw, you don't suppose she's married, do you? She must be. That kid is hers. Is the spitting image of her."

This observation seemed to put a momentary damper on the ardent bachelors at the window.

"He does have the look of her."

"Guys," Evan finally called, beyond impatience, "would you give it a rest?"

A few of them turned and acknowledged him with grins that were not in the least contrite, but basically they ignored him.

He did his best to shut them out.

But it penetrated his gloom about potty-training when one of them said, "I guess Mr. High and Mighty over there wouldn't care that the kid is looking at his truck."

Evan rattled the magazine. So what if someone was looking at his truck? It was a damned attractive truck, far worthier of a fuss than a strange woman passing through town.

"Guess old Mr. Lonesome over there wouldn't care, either, that the boy's looking over his shoulder right now. I don't like the look on his face, either, not one little bit."

Evan pretended he wasn't listening, but the truth was

they had his attention now. He was pretty protective of that truck. A fact they all knew. They were probably ribbing him a bit, trying to get him over there at the window to moan and groan over a complete stranger, just like them.

"It looks like he's writing something on it."

Well, okay, he hadn't been through the car wash for a while. Maybe the kid was writing a message in the dust. Big deal. Hardly headlines. Not even for Hopkins Gulch.

"Is that a nail he's using?" Sookie asked, amazed.

"I do believe it might be. Oh, that's an *S* for sure," Jack said.

Evan was up out of his booth now.

"Yup. And that's an *H*."

Evan crossed the café in one long stride and shoved his way through the guys to the front of the window. Just in time to see the little creep putting the finishing touches on an *I*. On his brand-new midnight-blue Dodge Ram Diesel extended cab pickup truck.

The guys were all staring at him, silent, horrified, knowing that that unsuspecting child's life as he knew it was about to end.

He pushed back through them and went out the door and across the dusty street in about one-tenth of a second.

The kid didn't even have time to put a dot on that *I*. Evan spun him around, and shoved him hard against his truck.

He was only about twelve. A good-looking boy, even though his features were contorted with fear and anger.

"What the hell do you think you're doing to my truck?" Evan demanded.

The boy sputtered and squirmed and began to turn red, but he didn't give anything that could qualify as an answer, so Evan twisted his shirt just a little tighter.

"Unhand that boy at once."

The voice was soft, sultry as silk, and with just a hint of pure steel in it.

Evan kept his grip on the boy's shoulder but spun on the heel of his cowboy boot to find himself staring into the most gorgeous set of brown eyes he had ever seen.

His first thought, foolishly, was they'd been wrong. All the guys had been wrong. There wasn't anything he'd ever seen in a Saturday night movie that even came close to this.

She was beautiful, her hair long and dark brown like melted chocolate, pulled back into a stern ponytail that ended between her shoulder blades. Her skin was the color of a peach, and had blushes in all the right places. Her eyes were so dark they were almost black, some flicker of anger in them hinting at a nature more hot and passionate than the primly buttoned lace-collared blouse was saying. Her cheekbones were high and proud, but her nose was a dainty, tiny thing, with a funny little smattering of freckles across it, and her lips were full and luscious and practically begged for kisses.

Begged.

But he was a man who had paid an enormous price for not saying no the last time lips had begged for kisses, and so his voice was frosty when he answered her.

"Ma'am?" he said.

"I said take your hands off my boy. What do you think you're doing?"

He shook his head, trying to think what he was doing, trying to shake the vision of her away so he could think clearly.

Her boy.

Vandalizing his truck. That was it.

"Yeah, take your hands off of me," the boy said, sneering.

Reluctantly he did.

The boy smirked, brushed at his sleeves deliberately, and then, like something unfolding in slow motion, reached over and wrapped his fist around the truck antenna. Before Evan could even think, he'd snapped it off.

Fury, hot and red, rose in Evan, not just because of the boy's flagrant lack of respect for his property but because of the soft gasp of shock and horror he heard from the woman. He shot her a quick glance and was dismayed by the transformation in her.

Cold, angry beauty he could handle with one hand tied behind his back. But now she was fundamentally altered as she stared at her child as if he had turned into a monster before her eyes. There was the faintest glitter of tears, of embarrassment and dismay, in eyes that he suddenly saw were not all brown, but partly gold. Her full bottom lip was trembling. And then she caught a glimpse of the nice letters scratched out with a nail in his brand-new paint, and he watched the color drain from her face.

"How could you?" she whispered to her boy.

"It wasn't hard at all, Auntie Kathy," the boy snapped at her, with disrespect that made Evan angrier, if that was even possible, than the damage that had been done to his truck. Even so he registered the "Auntie." She was not the young hellion's mother.

By now most of the guys from the café had gathered around and were watching with unabashed interest, nudging each other with satisfaction now that the kid had pushed Evan a little further.

Evan knew he had a well-deserved name as Hopkins Gulch's bad boy. He was a man with a reputation. Tough as nails. Cold as steel. Wild as the winter wind. A man who wasn't pushed. Quick to anger. Quick to take a dare. Quick to settle things with his fists. Quick to just about anything, if it came to that.

And he knew he looked the same as he always had, so these men he had grown up with assumed he was the same.

But he was not.

The wildest boy in town had wound up with the wildest girl in the world. Nothing less than he deserved. But the child had deserved something else. The change in Evan had begun the day his son had been born.

And deepened with every day that his boy had been missing.

Evan moved toward the kid. He had no intention of hurting him, would be satisfied to throw a scare into him good enough that he'd be an old man in a rocking chair before he ever messed with another man's truck.

But for a moment, his eyes locked on the boy's and he saw something. Something he didn't want to see. He skidded to a halt, and stared at those large gray eyes.

There was defiance in them, for sure. And a little deeper than that, fear.

And a little deeper than that…there was need. Need so raw and naked it killed the anger dead within Evan.

He ran a hand through his hair, and looked at the woman, a mistake, since it only confused him more.

"You just passing through?" he asked her, hopefully. She couldn't possibly be planning to stay here— a tiny spec on the map, an equally long distance from either Medicine Hat, Alberta, or Swift Current, Saskatchewan.

She dragged her gaze away from the boy who was sullenly inspecting the toe of his sneakers. "Actually, no. I've been hired at the Outpost. Of course, I'll pay for the damage to your truck. Right now. I'll—" She started fumbling with her pocketbook. "I'll write you a check. If you'll accept one from an out-of-town bank, for now. I—"

"No." Evan almost had to look over his shoulder, so dumbfounded was he that the emphatic no had issued forth from his mouth.

Because he *knew,* absolutely, that the thing to do was take her check.

Or let the cops handle it.

He *needed* to be in his nice new truck, driving away from her. Fast.

"No?" she repeated, the pocketbook hanging open, her hand frozen in its desperate search for a checkbook.

"No," he repeated, knowing he was going to do it. The good thing, the decent thing. Damn, sometimes it was hard. The easiest thing in the world was to be a self-centered SOB. He knew; he'd had lots of practice.

But if Dee had run forever with Jesse, if she hadn't died in an accident, this could be his boy standing here, nine or ten years in the future. If Evan was going to be the father his son deserved, he had to learn to do the right thing. Every time.

He suddenly felt calm and detached and like a voice deep within him, a voice he had learned to respect long ago, when the bull charged, when the brakes failed, when the thermometer registered thirty below and the cows still had to eat, when his son was gone and he just needed to get through one more day without losing his mind, that voice was telling him what to do.

He addressed the boy, low and firm, like he talked to a green colt, who was rebellious and scared, but wanted, in his heart, to know nothing more than he could trust you and you would never hurt him. "That five seconds of fun you just had is going to cost you about two weeks of moving manure. School's out for the year, right?"

"What?" the boy sputtered. "Why would I move manure for you?"

"Because you owe me, and that particular subject apparently holds some fascination for you since you feel inclined to write about it on the sides of people's trucks."

There was a murmur of surprise from the assembled crowd. Evan knew he was considered a man of few words, and most of those unprintable. But he heard the approval there, too, in the way he'd handled it.

"I'm not moving no manure." Only the boy didn't say manure.

Evan knew he had enough on his plate. His own son was just about to turn three, a stranger to his daddy, still in diapers, still sucking a soother, still crying himself silly if he got separated from his toy purple truck. Add to that a farm to run, doing his best to cook nutritious meals, laundry to do...how could he even be thinking of taking on anything else?

"Yes, you are." That was his voice, all right. His horse breakin' voice. Calm. Steady. Sure. A voice that did not brook defiance, from animal, nor man. Nor child.

"Make me."

"All right."

The boy's aunt finally spoke. Evan hazarded a look at her and saw, to his relief, her bottom lip had stopped quivering. Hopefully she wasn't going to cry. Her voice was soft, like velvet, the kind of voice that could bring a weak man to his knees.

Something he had learned his lesson from already, thank God, being weakened by feminine wiles.

"Moving manure?" she said uncertainly. "But we don't even know you."

He stuck out his hand. "Evan Atkins," he said.

"Kathleen Miles," she returned, accepting his hand with some reluctance.

Her hand in his was about the softest thing he'd ever felt, and he snatched his out of her grasp after one brief pump.

"Now we know each other," he said. He heard the cold note in his voice, turning it to ice, and recognized it was a defense against the sudden racing of his heart. Wouldn't do for her to know about that, no sir. She looked as if she was going to protest, but he cut her off. "Where's the boy's folks?"

"I'm his folks," she said stiffly.

"And you'll be working at the Outpost, for the Watsons?"

"Yes."

"You can ask them if it's safe for your boy to come work for me. They'll tell you."

"Oh."

He turned again to the boy. "And your name?"

"None of your business!"

"Okay, none-of-your-business, I'll pick you up right

here at five-thirty tomorrow morning. If you make me come looking, you'll be sorry, you hear?''

He noted the boy's aunt looked astounded when he offered a sullen ''I hear.'' Apparently thinking he'd given in too easily, the boy then added the word he had nearly succeeded in printing on the side of the truck.

She gasped again, but Evan just smiled and leaned close to the little delinquent. ''If I ever hear you say that word again, I'll wash out your mouth with Ma Watson's homemade lye soap. You can't believe how bad it tastes.''

Ma Watson, five foot one, in a man's shirt, with her gray hair neatly braided down her back, had appeared on the sidewalk. She chortled now, and said, ''And if anyone would know it would be you, Evan Atkins. Seems to me we went through a little stage where I felt it was my personal obligation to this town to have you spitting suds every ten minutes or so.''

Her comment broke the tension, and a ripple of laughter went through the assembled crowd, or as close as Hopkins Gulch ever came to a ''crowd.'' They began to disperse.

''Evan,'' Ma said, sweetly, ''can you show Kathleen over to her house? I just had a customer come in.''

Evan glanced at the store, pretty sure the door had not swung inward in the last ten minutes or so. Still, he couldn't very well call Ma a liar in front of her new employee, and besides, for all she sounded sweet, she had just given an order, drill sergeant to buck private.

The old gal had really done more than anyone else in this town to try to show a boy going wild the difference between right and wrong, and enough of her tough caring had penetrated his thick skull to keep him out of jail over the years.

Once, when he was sixteen, she had said to him, "Evan, each man has two knights within him, a knight of lightness and a knight of darkness. The one you feed the most will become the strongest."

At sixteen, he had found the words laughable, thought they had gone in one ear and out the other. But in actual fact, those words had stopped somewhere between those two ears, and for some reason now, ten years later, he found himself contemplating them, embarrassed almost by his longing to choose the right one.

"Evan?" Ma said.

Besides, Medicine Hat was a long haul for groceries. "Yes, ma'am," he said, "I'll show her the house." He assumed that meant have a quick look around inside and make sure a rattlesnake hadn't cozied up in some dark corner for the winter. He also assumed Ma wouldn't want him to share that little fact of life in Hopkins Gulch with her new employee just yet.

"Kathleen, dear, you take your time getting settled. Let Evan and the boy bring the heavy stuff in. I'll see you here at the store tomorrow."

Evan took a deep breath, intending to point out that showing Miss Miles the little empty house Ma owned, three blocks from here, and moving her into it were really two separate tasks. One look at Ma and he bit his tongue.

Why was it that woman could turn him into a twelve-year-old with his hand caught in her candy jar in a single glance? Why was it she made him want to be the white knight? A joke, really. He was just a farmer, and part-time cowboy, in muddy boots and torn jeans. He turned on the heel of one of those boots, got in his truck and watched in the rearview mirror as the beautiful Miss Miles herded the boy into her car and pulled in behind him.

She had a beautiful figure, full and lush, a figure that could make a man like himself, sworn off women, reconsider, start to think thoughts of soft curves and warm places.

Evan, he told himself, it only leads one place. It starts with an innocent thought: I wonder what it would be like to kiss her. The next thing you know, *Potty-Training for the Hopelessly Confused*. He realized he left his damned book in the café, and hoped that Millie possessed enough mercy to hide it for him until he had a chance to get back in there and pick it up.

He was angry, Kathleen thought, as she pulled to a stop behind him, and watched him hop out of his truck.

Well, who could blame him? The most noticeable thing about his vehicle now was the two-foot high *S H I* printed on the side of it.

Still, she didn't have much experience dealing with angry men. And certainly not ones who looked like this. Even with that menacing scowl on his face as he waited on the sidewalk outside the gate of a yard, Evan Atkins was gorgeous.

He looked like a young Redford, with his corn silk and wheat colored hair, though his grayish-blue eyes held none of Redford's boyish charm, only a hard and intimidating hint of ice and iron. His features were chiseled masculine perfection—high cheekbones, straight nose, wide mouth, firm lips, a strong chin.

He was average height, maybe five-eleven, but the breadth of his chest and shoulders had left her with the impression of strength and leashed power. He was narrow at his stomach and hip, and his long, blue jean-encased legs looked as if they'd wrapped themselves around a lot of horses. And probably quite a few other things, too.

Kathleen decided Evan Atkins was not a safe man for her to be around. Lately she had noticed that her mind wandered off in distinctly naughty directions with barely the slightest provocation. Part of being old, she was sure. Not just old, but an old spinster.

She was kidding herself. It was because of Howard announcing his intention to marry someone else. Hope quashed.

"Thank you," she called to him, half in and half out of her car. "Is that the house? I can manage now."

He didn't budge.

The house was hidden behind a tall hedge. Throughout the long drive here she had been so eager to see the accommodations that came with her new job. Now she had to get past the guard at the gate. Now she wasn't nearly as interested in that house as she had been a thousand miles ago. He had a kind of energy about him that made everything else seem to fade into the distance, uninteresting and unimportant.

"Three days is too long to drive," she muttered to herself.

"Auntie Kathy, you're getting old," Mac informed her, an unfortunate confirmation of her own thoughts. "You're talking to yourself." He glanced at the man standing at the gate, wriggled deeper into his seat in the car and turned a page of his comic book.

She made herself get all the way out of the car, and walk toward Evan.

"Really," she said, "Thank you. You don't have to—"

He held open the gate for her. The opening was far too narrow to get by him. She practically touched him. She caught a whiff of something headier than the lilacs blooming in wild profusion around the yard.

"I'm sorry about your truck," she said, nervously. "Mac decided he was going to hate it here the minute I told him we were moving. I think he can get himself run out of town on a rail."

"I guess if this town could survive me as a twelve-year-old, it'll survive him."

She realized she liked his voice, deep and faintly drawling, and something else.

"How did you know? Twelve?"

"Just a guess. Where are you coming from, ma'am?"

She realized what the "something else" was in his voice. It was just plain sexy. The way he said ma'am, soft and dragged out at the end, made her tingle down to her toes. She snuck a glance at him. It occurred to her he was younger than she. That should have made his raw masculine potency less threatening, somehow, but it didn't.

"Vancouver," she said. "We're relocating from Vancouver."

"That's one hell of a relocate."

"Yes, I know." Though he didn't ask, she felt, absurdly, that she had to defend herself. "The ad for the position at the Outpost said this was a great place to raise a family."

He snorted at that.

"Isn't it?" she asked, desperately.

"Ma'am, I'm the wrong person to ask about families."

"Oh." She snuck a glance over his broad shoulder

at the house, and tried not to feel disappointed. It was very old, the whole thing covered in dreadful gray asphalt shingles. The porch looked droopy.

Feeling as if she was trying to convince herself she had not made a horrible mistake, she said, "Vancouver is starting to have incidents with gangs. There are problems in the schools. Children as young as Mac are becoming involved in alcohol and drugs."

Of course she was not going to tell him the whole truth, her life story. That her boss, Howard, whom she'd once been engaged to, was going to marry someone else.

A little smile twisted his lips. "You don't say?"

She bristled. "You're not suggesting my nephew might be involved in such things just because of that incident with your truck, are you?"

"No, ma'am. I don't know the first thing about your nephew, except he seems to have a talent for spelling. But I know I wasn't much older than that when I first sampled a little home brew, right here in Hopkins Gulch."

She stared at him, aghast.

"Kids as wild as I was find trouble no matter where they are," he said, apparently by way of reassurance.

"And are you still wild, Mr. Atkins?" she asked. Too late, she realized she sounded as prissy as an old maid librarian.

He seemed to contemplate that for a moment, his eyes intent on her. "Life has tamed me some."

There was something vaguely haunted in the way he said that, something that made him seem altogether too intriguing, as if the steel and ice in his eyes had been earned the hard way.

She reminded herself, sternly, that she was completely unavailable to solve the puzzle of mysterious men, no matter how compelling they might be. She had a boy to raise. When her sister had died, Kathleen had vowed she would give that job her whole heart and soul. Howard had broken their engagement over her decision, and after that she had decided that Mac didn't need the emotional upheaval that seemed to be part and parcel of relationships.

It really wasn't until Howard had announced his engagement a month ago at the office that she had realized she had held the hope that he would change his mind, or maybe even that he was waiting for Mac to grow up, that later would be *their* turn.

What had she thought? That he would wait until she was really old? And probably saggy, too?

Like this old house. She forced herself to look away from Atkins, to take note of the yard that was now hers. Behind it, through a hedge of more lilac, Kathleen could see the prairie, huge, undulating, without a tree or a shrub or a flower for as far as the eye could see. The yard itself was ringed with blooming lilac bushes. The flower beds had been long neglected and the grass was too high, but the yard was large and private and she could tell just a little bit of tender loving care could make it lovely. There was the garden space, at the side of the house. She took a deep breath of the lilac-scented air.

"What is that smell?" Mac asked, catapulting through the gate.

"Lilacs," Kathleen told him.

"I think I'm allergic."

"Mrs. Watkins told me there's a pasture right on the other side of the hedge if you happen to decide you want a pony," Kathleen said, hoping to find one thing he could like and look forward to.

"A pony?" he said, giving her a slightly distressed look, as if she had landed on earth after being hatched on a distant planet. "Is that, like, a brand of skateboard?"

She saw Evan duck his head, but not before she saw the quick grin. It changed his face, completely. Completely. He had beautiful teeth and deep dimples. He could look very boyishly attractive, after all.

"A pony," she snapped. "Like a horse."

"I'm allergic to horses, too," Mac decided, and then added, sending Evan a sidelong look, "And also manure."

Evan ignored him. "I'll just take a quick look inside the house for you."

"Why?"

"It's been empty a spell, I think. You never know what might have taken up residence."

She stared at him in horror. "Such as?"

"You never know," he repeated, deliberately unforthcoming.

"Like a homeless tramp?" she asked unsteadily.

"No," he said, his mouth quirking reluctantly upward at one corner. "Hopkins Gulch doesn't have any homeless tramp problems."

"Mice?" she pressed.

"Well, I was thinking of, uh, skunks, but sure, mice."

She scanned his face, suspecting he wasn't telling her the full truth.

"I'll bet that place is full of mice," Mac said, sensing a weakness. "I'll bet they'll be running over our faces at night when we try to sleep. I'll bet we'll find little paw prints in the butter. I'll bet there are dinky round holes in the baseboards, just like in the cartoons. I'll bet the only thing that keeps the mice under control are the skunks. I'll bet—''

"I'd say that's enough bets," Evan said quietly, glancing at her face.

Mac looked mutinous. "It's a very old house. Probably even older than you, Auntie Kathy.''

She felt Evan's gaze on her face, again, but he made no comment on her age in relation to the house.

Mac flopped down on the grass, rolled his eyes, grabbed his throat and began gagging. Whether it was in reaction to the lilacs or the house she decided it would be wise not to ask. Following Evan's lead, she ignored Mac who was now writhing dramatically, and went up the creaking steps.

The door swung open, and her first impression was one of gloom. Fighting not to show her disappointment, she followed Evan through the empty house. He was wearing a chambray shirt and faded jeans. This back view showed off the broadness of his shoulders to breathtaking advantage. The jeans were soft with wear and hugged the taut line of his backside and the firm muscle of his leg. He made all the rooms seem too small. He'd brought that smell right in with him—clean skin, faint aftershave, man-smell.

He opened the closets and looked through the cupboards. She didn't follow him into the basement, but he came back up the stairs, and proclaimed her new home varmint free.

Mac, obviously disappointed that his lilac-induced collapse on the front lawn had failed to convince anyone of his distress, came through the door, a sour expression on his face.

"What a dump," he proclaimed. "This whole town is like the dumpiest dump that I've ever seen and I hate it here."

Evan ignored him. "Ma'am, do you need a hand with your things?"

This was offered only politely.

"No, thanks," she said proudly.

She wanted the man out of her house. So she could concentrate. So that she could deal with Mac, figure out what had to be done to make the place livable, and then shut herself in the bathroom and cry.

Chapter Two

"Thank you for giving it a fair chance," she said icily to Mac, after Evan had left. "I cannot believe you behaved like that. Broke Mr. Atkins's antenna off his truck, wrote that word. What on earth has gotten into you?"

Mac looked at his toe, clad in expensive sneakers that he *had* to have, and that seemed to have brought him joy and contentment for exactly ten seconds, and then shoved his hands deep into his pockets before he shot her a look loaded with defiance. "I hate it here, that's why. I want to go home."

"This is going to be home," Kathleen said with determination. Her eyes were adjusting to the gloom in the room, and she noticed the floors were old gray linoleum, peeling back in places, the walls needed paint desperately, there were spiderwebs in the corners. She went over and tugged at a blind. It rolled up with a snap, and the sunlight poured into the empty room, but did nothing to improve it. *This* was going to be home?

She thought of her and Mac's cozy little apartment in Vancouver and felt heartsick.

"You won't believe how rotten I can be," Mac warned her.

She let none of her own doubts show. She said calmly, "Then you will just have to get very good at shoveling manure. I'll bet there is no shortage of that around here."

"Well, you got that right," Mac said heatedly. "How could you do this to me? You've ruined my whole life. Me. Mac Miles in Poop Gulch, Saskatchewan." Only he didn't say poop.

"The first thing I'm going to do at work tomorrow is find out about that soap," Kathleen said.

"And what am I supposed to do while you're at work?"

"You already sorted that out, Mac. You'll be shoveling manure." Only she didn't say manure, either.

He stared at her, obviously stunned that his aunt would use that word. He changed directions swiftly. "I suppose you thought that guy was good-looking."

And for the briefest moment, she saw the little boy in him, and saw how scared he was. He was sad and scared and he was too anxious to be a man to say so.

"Oh, Mac, come here."

He came, and even allowed her to put her arms around him and she found herself saying, "Everything will be fine." With him snuggled against her, those words felt true, and it actually did feel as if it could be home here.

Mac tolerated her embrace for three seconds or so, then pulled away and walked down the narrow hall. "I guess I'll have this room," he said after a minute.

"Auntie Kathy, you never answered me. Did you think that dust hopper was good-looking?"

"Dust hopper?"

"The goof with the truck."

She didn't answer, appalled by this creature who was her nephew.

"I thought he was real ugly," Mac said. "Real. And way too young for you. *Way.*" He slammed his bedroom door.

She thought of him sitting in that empty room, nursing his own bad humor, and sighed. She looked around again at her homely house, and went into the bathroom. More aging linoleum. She thought of Evan Atkins being *way* too young for her, and him not even commenting, when he'd been given the opportunity, that the house was obviously years older than she was.

Howard's new fiancée was young, blond, perky.

You broke up with him five years ago, Kathleen reminded herself savagely. You're over it. She barely locked the door before the tears started to fall.

It had been a stupid thing to do, to take a job in a place she had never heard of. Stupid, stupid. Stupid. When she'd been hired sight unseen, when that letter had arrived, she'd actually thought, naively, whimsically, that it had been heaven sent. She had told herself this was her chance to start anew. To be somebody new. Somebody who worried less and laughed more. Who did daring and bold things—like moved to a town they had never heard of.

Kathleen allowed herself to snivel for ten minutes, and then came out, knocked firmly on Mac's bedroom door and told him they had a great deal of work to do to make this house into their home.

Stupid or not, they were here, and she had to make the best of it.

She unlocked the U-haul and after some rummaging handed Mac a broom. When he rolled his eyes, she said, "Be thankful it's not a shovel."

"I don't like this house," Mac said.

"It didn't live up to my expectations, either," she admitted, "but I can make it clean, and in time it'll be cute, too."

"Oh, *cute*." He shot her a sideways glance. "Did you think *he* was? Cute?"

"No," she said, "not at all."

Her response was completely honest. Evan Atkins *cute?* It would be like calling a grizzly bear adorable. Howard had been cute with his big brown eyes, his curly hair, his little potbelly.

Mac was clearly relieved with her answer.

She spent the rest of the day feverishly cleaning the little house from top to bottom, scrubbing walls and floors and appliances. Mac was surprisingly helpful, but only until his boom box came out of the trailer. By nightfall, Kathleen had only the energy left to move in two mattresses and a box of bedding.

"You don't have to get up with me in the morning," Mac told her. "You look really tired." When she got up in the morning, he was gone, but he had found the coffeepot and made coffee for her. Just when she was about to lose hope in him, he would win her back by doing something sweet and thoughtful like that.

She walked the three blocks to work, noting they comprised most of the town. She spent the day at the Outpost, learning the inventory, which was extensive, and prices, and how to use the archaic cash register.

She was amazed by the number of people who came

through the store, until Ma told her they were coming from miles around to check her out. She was asked on six dates before noon! It did wonders for her flagging spirits, even if she did say no to all of them.

At four she headed home, exhausted, knowing she had that U-haul to unload. Still, she had all the ingredients for Mac's favorite spaghetti supper, and couldn't wait to fill up that little house with the good smells of garlic and tomatoes and pasta.

But by five o'clock Mac still wasn't home.

She scanned the road yet again. She thought she had heard a truck, but it proved to be a large farm vehicle.

Mac had left at five this morning. Twelve hours? Didn't that seem a little long to work a twelve-year-old?

It occurred to her he might have been in an accident.

She laughed nervously at that. It would be the worst of ironies if she moved from busy Vancouver to sleepy Saskatchewan, mostly for Mac's sake, only to have him maimed or killed in an accident.

Of course, she had never actually seen Evan pick him up. What if he had gone to the highway and hitch-hiked away? What if even now—

Stop, she ordered herself. This was what her book on positive thinking said she must not do, think in negatives, create whole scenes and scenarios. The book, she recalled, instructed her to try to turn her negative thoughts around, to think now, of something positive.

She tried to picture Mac having a wonderful day. She pictured him on a farm. She pictured him chasing through tall grass after a butterfly, having just the kind of day she had pictured when she'd applied for this job.

She went back and stirred the spaghetti sauce. Why had she made so much?

Kathleen Miles, you are not inviting that man in for dinner.

Just then she heard a truck pull up. She set down the spoon in such a hurry it splattered sauce on her white blouse. She ran to the front window.

The right truck. She went out of the house and onto the porch.

Mac got out of it and slammed the door. He marched up the walk, his back straight, his clothes absolutely filthy, a pungent aroma following him.

She glanced anxiously at his running shoes.

Clean.

"How was it?" she asked him.

"How do you think?" he snapped.

"Oh."

"Hey, none-of-your-business." Evan Atkins had gotten out of his truck and was coming down the walk toward them.

Mac turned and glared at him.

"Same time, same place," Evan said.

Mac gave him a dirty look and when it didn't phase Evan, he gave it to her instead. Then he muttered a word she couldn't quite make out and the porch door slammed shut behind him.

Evan Atkins continued down the walk toward her.

She tucked a strand of hair behind her ear, and suddenly felt very aware of the little splotch of spaghetti sauce on the front of her. She wasn't going to let him see that she felt vulnerable!

He walked with the easy assurance of a man completely comfortable within his own body, a man sure of himself. His self-certainty annoyed her even more in the face of her own lack of it.

"I wish you wouldn't call him none-of-your-business," she said, far more sharply than she intended, sounding exactly like the aging spinster she was. "His name is Mac."

"Actually, I know that. I'm just waiting for the invitation to come from him."

His voice was low and calm, a faint thread of amusement running through it, though he wasn't smiling. Did he find her amusing? Probably that spaghetti splotch. He stopped, rested one foot on her bottom step and looked up at her.

"Where on earth have you been?" Her voice was still sharper than she intended, but definitely the tone of a woman who planned to be taken seriously.

His eyes widened. "Ma'am?"

His eyes were dark ocean-blue, with flecks of the most intriguing gray.

"He left at five-thirty this morning!"

"My place is a good half hour drive from here, ma'am. That's an hour round trip. I had a lot of work to do today. I couldn't just stop everything to drive him back into town when he thought he'd had enough. Which was about five minutes after he started."

"Twelve hours is a long time for a little boy to work."

"He's not that little. Besides, we stopped for lunch."

"I don't even think it's legal to work a man that long!"

"Well, ma'am," he said, a bit of a fire lighting in those cool ocean eyes, "if it makes you feel any better, we didn't even make a dent in that anger he's carrying around."

"Mac is not angry!" She had no idea why she said that, when it was so pathetically obvious he was.

"Scratching that particular word in the side of a person's truck can't exactly be interpreted as 'I come in peace.'"

"I don't think he better work for you tomorrow."

"Now, ma'am, it's really none of my business, but I think that would be a mistake."

"Really?" she said haughtily.

"I don't think you want to be teaching that boy that he can behave any old way he likes, and that there won't be any consequences for it. Mama Bear will bail him out."

He was right, and they both knew it.

Still, she couldn't seem to stop herself from saying, "And you're an expert on raising children, are you?"

She was sorry the minute she said it, knowing she was taking out all her anxiety about her move and Mac on him, and that he didn't deserve it. Besides, as soon as she said it, in his eyes she caught a glimpse of a pain that was as raw as an open wound.

But his voice was steady, and completely unflappable. He answered slowly, measuring his words. "No, I'm sure not that. It just seems to me if you bail him out now, you'll be bailing him out in quite a different way in the future."

She took a deep breath, realized she was being both cranky and unfair and that he was right and she was wrong. She was completely unable to admit that. "I was worried about him. I was worried when he was gone so long."

It was Evan's look of genuine distress that soothed some of the irritation she had been feeling.

"I didn't mean to cause you worry. I guess I should

have called.'' He smiled, shook his head and said, ''I feel like I've said those words a few times before in my life.''

She just bet he had. Those charming dimples had probably won the hearts of hundreds of women who had waited by their phones with bated breath for his call. That never came. She planned never to be one of them. Never. That was one very good reason she couldn't invite him to share spaghetti with them.

''I guess I thought I'd keep him out of your hair while you were at work,'' he said.

He'd been doing her a favor, or thought he was, and she was giving him a hard time about it?

''He's not such a bad kid,'' she said defensively, and then realized, suddenly, how ridiculous she must seem—a mother bear protecting her cub, just as he had said.

''Ma'am, I can see that.''

''You can?''

His smile deepened and she was now certain she did not like his smile. It made him, in an instant, in to one of those men who can have anything. Anything. Had she really cooked that dinner just for Mac? Was she feeling prickly as a pear because her nerves were leaping with awareness of this attractive stranger resting his boot-clad foot on her front step?

''In the odd moment. I had him bring the mix out to my calves. I wish you could have seen the look on his face.''

''I wish I could have seen that, too.''

''Well, maybe you will one time.''

''Thanks. Maybe I will.'' But since that would mean tangling her life a little more with Evan Atkins she decided she wouldn't. She had pinned her hopes on

Howard, and he had let her down, and the hurt was terrible.

And Howard wasn't nearly as...compelling as the young, and gorgeous Mr. Atkins. In fact, Howard suddenly seemed very blah, boring. If a blah and boring man could hurt her so much she really didn't want to think what an exciting and passionate one could do.

"How did things go your first day on the job?"

"Oh. Fine." What made her think he was passionate? The smoky look in his eyes? The uncomplicated sensuality of his lips?

"Everybody within a hundred miles dropped by to say howdy?"

She felt some of the stiffness leave her and she laughed. "A thousand, I think."

"Ma'am, I wouldn't be surprised."

"Quit calling me ma'am!" Why did her tone have to be so querulous with him? "Please."

"All right." He waited.

She blushed, as if she had just turned sixteen and not thirty-four. "Kathleen."

"Well, Kathleen, I'll bet your dance card is full right up for the next year or so."

"Pardon?"

"They all ask you out? The bachelors of Hopkins Gulch?"

"Oh. A few of them. I don't do that. Go out."

"You don't? Why not?"

Why not? There was no Howard to be loyal to anymore. What kind of woman was loyal to a man for five years after he'd broken up with her? A dolt, that's what kind.

"I don't think it would be good for Mac."

"How's that?"

"In my experience—" admittedly limited, though she didn't say that "—romance seems to be distinctly upsetting."

"Distinctly upsetting," he repeated thoughtfully. "I'd have to go along with you on that one. By the way, does Mac really have allergies? To horses?"

"No. Did he tell you that?"

"Deathly, according to him. One whiff of horse and immediate anaphylactic reaction. Said he forgot his kit at home. Like a beesting kit, only a horse whiff kit."

She was staring at Evan trying to hide her horror. When had her nephew become such an accomplished liar? She didn't even know Mac knew the word anaphylactic.

"I take it," Evan said at her silence, "it would be quite safe to have him feed the horses tomorrow?"

"Quite safe," she murmured.

"If he comes."

"He'll come."

"I'll be here at five-thirty, then."

"All right."

He turned and walked away. She was fascinated by the way he walked, loose-limbed and confident, like a man who owned the earth.

"So, what should I call you?" she called after him.

He stopped and looked back at her. "This is a pretty casual kind of place. Evan would do fine."

"Thanks, Evan, for looking after his shoes." Was she actually trying to keep him here? If she didn't watch herself, she'd be inviting him in for supper in a minute.

He gave her a lopsided grin that chased the shadows from his face and made him look charming and boyish and about a hundred years younger than she.

"Did you really pay two hundred dollars for those shoes?"

"Not quite," she said, "but close."

He shook his head incredulously. "Why?"

"They're magic shoes," she said with a sigh. "They were supposed to make him happy."

"If you got that in writing, I'd take them back." He turned then, went down the walk and got into his truck.

She had to bite her tongue to keep herself from stopping him one more time, asking him if he'd like to join them for spaghetti.

It wouldn't be a date. Not even close. Just a neighborly kind of thing.

Not wanting to look pathetic, she did not watch while he drove away.

She went into the house just as Mac came out of the shower, toweling his head. The freckles had darkened across his nose, and his cheeks were full of color from the sun.

"I really hate that dust hopper," he told her. "I worked hard enough today that I shouldn't have to go back."

"Well, you do," Kathleen said, glad that her resolve had been strengthened by her talk with Evan.

"He worked me really hard, and didn't give me enough to eat or drink. I think there are laws against treating kids like that."

"There are laws about damaging people's property," she said sternly. She tried to get him to think positive, just as the book said. "Tell me one good thing that happened to you today."

He scowled at her. "There wasn't one."

"Oh, come on. Tell me about the calves."

"They're really stupid and they stink. Just like his kid."

"His kid?" Kathleen asked, stunned.

"Yeah. He has a little boy named Jesse. He's nearly three and he wears diapers. Is that normal?"

"I'm not sure."

"He doesn't talk much, especially when the Gestapo is around."

"Who doesn't talk much? And what Gestapo?"

"The baby doesn't talk much. And the Gestapo is the dust hopper you think is so cute."

"I never said I thought he was cute." She was sure she was going to blush and give herself away, so she turned quickly. Over her shoulder she said, "Don't call him that again. Gestapo. That's dreadful."

"Well, so is shoveling for no pay. That kid can't say *r*. Is that normal?"

"I don't know." Why was it making her feel so inadequate that she couldn't answer his questions? Making her feel as if she had missed something. A baby of her own. Another dream Howard had stolen from her. If she waited until Mac was grown up, another six years at least, wouldn't it be too late then? She'd be forty!

"It doesn't seem normal. He says wabbit for rabbit. Could I say *r?*"

"I don't ever remember you not saying *r*."

"That's good because it sounds really stupid."

"Where's Jesse's mom?"

"She died in a *caw*."

"Oh, Mac."

"It really stinks, doesn't it, when mom's die and leave their kids? At least he has a dad who cares about him, even if he is the Gestapo."

Spoken carelessly, it failed to hide his pain. He was still grieving the loss of his mother, even though it had been nearly five years now. And his father. Kathleen felt a nameless fury. He'd never even seen his son. Abandoned her sister and his unborn child as soon as he'd learned she was pregnant.

And of course, then there had been Howard, who had told her, shortly after her sister's death, "It's Mac or me." Not quite in those words, of course. Howard was always so good with words. Educated. Sophisticated. Things that had impressed her once.

"I care about you, Mac," she said firmly. "I love you more than a leopard loves its spots."

Mac couldn't resist the game. "I love you more than a toad loves its warts."

And suddenly the anger melted from his face, and he was just her sweet little boy again. And he said, "Did you make me spaghetti for supper?"

"Just for you." Why did that sound like a lie?

He smiled. "I love you more than a pizza loves pepperoni."

It seemed to Evan that all of life really turned on a hair. He glanced in the back seat, where Jesse was fast asleep in his car seat. A little puddle of drool was forming on the tiny Western shirt Jesse had spotted at the Outpost several days ago. It had been on a mannequin, and Jesse had stood in front of it, silent, his eyes large with wanting. It had broken Evan's heart that he didn't ask. He'd bought it for him anyway. Now he was having trouble getting the shirt off his son long enough to put it in the washer.

He looked back at the long ribbon of road and

thought, a choice made here, a split second there, and everything changes.

He'd met Dee at a rodeo, she a top-rated barrel racer in sequins and tight jeans, he a not so highly rated bull rider with quite a bit more nerve than talent. She had short blond curly hair and huge brown eyes, and a tiny china doll figure that belied the power she showed on a horse. She was without a doubt the most beautiful woman he had ever laid eyes on. She was also the only woman he'd ever met who could match him drink for drink, who could party all night and go all day. Maybe he should have taken that as a danger sign, but he hadn't.

Now, he wondered sometimes, if he'd gone to a different rodeo that day, or stayed at home, or had a flat tire, or taken a wrong turn, maybe he would have never met Dee. Maybe that little life in the back seat would have never happened.

All of life turned on these split-second decisions that a man had no hope of recognizing at the time he made them.

And here he was again.

His life turning on a hair.

If he hadn't been in town yesterday, his life wouldn't be intertwining with hers, with Kathleen Miles. If Mac had snapped off a different antenna, everything would be, well, different.

He wouldn't be driving home to his empty house, thinking about the smell that had been wafting out her open porch door. Something mouthwatering. Italian. And thinking about that U-haul out front, still as full as it had been yesterday.

"Evan, don't even think about turning this truck around," he ordered himself.

Just as firmly he told himself he was not thinking of Kathleen Miles romantically. Not at all. He was a man who had learned his lessons about romance. What had she said?

Oh, yeah. *Romance was distinctly upsetting.* Apparently she had learned her lessons, too.

So, why, if he had learned his lessons, had he been absolutely compelled to ask her if she'd been asked out? He knew she would have been. Those guys that had lined up three-deep at the café window yesterday would have lost no time in getting over to the Outpost to check her out today.

Her response to them was none of his business. None. Still, there was no denying he felt happy that they had all struck out with her.

Not, he thought darkly, that Sookie Peters was going to take no for an answer. Kathleen was too beautiful. Sookie would be back over at the Outpost tomorrow, probably with a little bouquet of flowers, and lots of sweet talk. Kathleen didn't date? That wouldn't be a problem for Sookie. He'd think of a way for it not to be a date.

In fact, Sookie probably wouldn't wait until tomorrow. He was probably at her place right now, unloading that U-haul, and getting himself invited in for a home-made dinner. That wouldn't be a date, would it? No, sir, that would just be being neighborly.

Dinner. Evan tried to think what he had at home that would qualify and hit all four food groups at the same time. Frozen pizza. Canned stew. Before Jesse he would have thought a food group was the fries next to the burger on his plate. But that lady lawyer in Swift Current had told him, when Dee's parents had been acting as if they were going to challenge him over guardianship, that he would have to be really aware of things like that. Nutrition. Child psychology.

He suddenly felt achingly lonely and overwhelmed.

"Don't you dare turn the truck around," he said to himself. "You can't just show up at a woman's house at dinnertime, hoping she'll feed you."

In exchange for unloading her U-haul, the other voice said indignantly.

The kind of thing a white knight might do, except a real knight wouldn't expect dinner.

Sighing, recognizing all life turned on a hair, and there was not a damn thing he could do about it, Evan Atkins slowed, stopped and turned his truck around.

He told himself that she looked like the kind of woman who might know a thing or two about potty-training.

Chapter Three

"Oh," Mac said, through the screen. "It's you. Auntie Kathy, Colonel Klink is here. And he brought Mr. Stinky Pants with him. Is Mr. Stinky Pants alive?"

"Yeah, he's just sleeping." Evan could feel his son's warm breath against his shoulder.

"Hi," Evan said, when she appeared at the door. Did she look pleased to see him? Even after that introduction?

"I'm sorry," she said, tossing an annoyed look back at Mac. She had a tea towel over her shoulder, and her hair was falling out of her ponytail and curling around her face. "Where does he come up with this stuff?"

The smells coming out that door were even more heavenly than before.

"Hogan's Heroes," Evan guessed. "Late night." He knew all about late nights.

"Is this your son?" A good sign. Not, *What are you doing back here?*

''Jesse,'' he said, ''otherwise known as Mr. Stinky Pants.''

She smiled and came out the door and looked at Jesse's sleeping face. She reached out and touched a blond curl.

''He's gorgeous,'' she said, her voice rich with tenderness, ''He's just like a little angel.''

A man could not be jealous of his three-year-old son. It was not permissible. Especially when he was not here about romance, heaven forbid. Simply being neighborly. Or a knight, however one wanted to look at it. Still, a man would probably go a long way to have a woman look at him with that kind of bone-melting sweetness.

''I was thinking if you had a place I could lay him down, I'd haul that stuff in from the trailer for you.''

''Oh,'' she said, and blushed.

Who would think a woman that age could blush? He tried to figure out her age. Older than him. Mid-thirties, maybe. One of those women who aged with uncommon grace, her body full and ripe, her face kind, her dark eyes steady and serene. Why was it women thought they needed to be forever young when he found this so appealing?

Women liked him. That had been a fact of his life for as long as he could remember. But it always seemed to be a certain kind that was attracted to him—young, full of breathless giggles and chatter, dyed blond hair and shirts that showed off their belly buttons. Women who didn't blush, and who seemed to like the word *cool* best out of the entire English language, who wore red, red lipstick and chewed gum. An evening with a woman like that left him feeling so empty and exhausted he'd pretty much given up on it. Especially now that Jesse was home.

But he could tell just by looking at her, just by looking at her eyes, that Kathleen Miles was a different sort of woman—one of those women who would truly keep getting better as she got older.

"That's very kind of you," she said. "Come in."

She held open the door for him. Underlying the smell of garlic and butter and onions, he could smell lemon-scented cleaner and window shine. And her.

No Poison or White Shoulders or Shalimar, just her, clean and fresh and real.

Her house was still practically empty, but spotless now, the walls dirt free, the floor sparkling, no dust motes or spiderwebs anywhere, not even in the corners. Evan thought of how the floors in his house had become a little bit sticky, handprints multiplying on his walls.

Mac had disappeared, but Evan could hear loud music from behind a closed door. "Don't go messin' with a son-of-a..." A song he'd practically considered his theme song ten years ago. Kids were still listening to it? And watching *Hogan's Heroes?* Maybe he and Mac had more in common than a two-story high pile of manure that had to be moved.

"In here," she said.

He followed her into a bedroom that only yesterday had seemed cold and empty and a bit ugly. Today it had her mattress in the middle of the floor, all neatly made up in white eyelet, so feminine and pretty it made his mouth go dry.

"I don't think I better put him on that." He thought of the rumple of sheets and blankets on his bed at home. When was the last time he'd made a bed?

"It washes," she said with a shrug.

In his house, "it washes" didn't necessarily mean it got washed. It got put in one of those piles that he did his best to ignore until he or Jesse started running out of stuff to wear.

He laid his son down on her bed, hoping the shirt that Jesse had had on for three days wouldn't leave any smudges on the pristine white of her bedspread. He noticed she had hung a white sheet over the window, and tied it back with a bow. It lifted with the breeze, and fluttered and made him think, irrationally, of things exotic and mysterious and feminine. How could those two small changes to the room make it feel so different than it had felt yesterday?

"I'll get your bed frame set up," he said. "You shouldn't be sleeping on the floor."

"I know," she said. "The mice will be running over my face."

He decided not to tell her the plus side of living in rattlesnake country. They did keep the rodent population under control.

"Would you like something to eat first? It's almost ready."

"Well," he hesitated, "if you insist."

She didn't even look suspicious! He followed her into the kitchen. It, too, hadn't had much done to it, though it sparkled with cleanliness. He thought if he moved every stick of furniture in his kitchen outside onto the lawn he could do this, too. Just bring in a garden hose and spray down the whole kitchen—blast the jam off the floor, the spots off the countertops, the grime off the stove, the fingerprints off the fridge. A good project for summertime, when the cattle were less work.

He looked out the window. Sookie Peters drove by, spotted his truck and kept going. He and Sookie had duked it out in Grade Eleven. Over Betty Sue Mc-Donald. He hadn't had to reestablish dominance since then.

Betty Sue had been real pretty. Smith, now. She and her husband lived in Swift Current. The last time he'd seen her he'd noticed how her prettiness was fading, petals falling off a rose.

No doubt about it. Kathleen Miles had a hardier kind of beauty, growing more lustrous, rather than fading, like those flowers that look their best in the autumn. Probably not one single person in her high school would have recognized that for what it was.

"Was that an old red truck driving by?" she asked from the stove.

"Hmm." Was she *expecting* Sookie?

"It's driven by here about half a dozen times. Do you think I should call the police?"

"Call the police?" he asked. "On Sookie?" Come to think of it, it might be kind of fun.

"On who?"

"Sookie Peters. He was probably one of the guys in the Outpost today trying to get your phone number."

"Oh! I thought it was some sort of weirdo. Maybe watching Mac."

It was tempting to brand Sookie as a weirdo, but the white knight, stronger now because he was going to do a good deed and move her furniture for her, gave him a little prod. "Kathleen, I know those kind of weirdos don't generally hang out signs, but I'm pretty sure we don't have any in Hopkins Gulch. You are one big city woman, aren't you?"

"I am. I grew up in Vancouver. Can you imagine? This is the first time I've been away."

She tested her spaghetti sauce, then held out the spoon to him.

It was a ridiculous thing to find sexy. Ridiculous. But when he put his lips on the spoon where hers had been he felt weak with pleasure.

Because of the spaghetti sauce, he told himself. "That's pretty good," he told her, an understatement. But if he said what he felt, *orgasmic,* she'd for sure think he was weirder than Sookie.

"More garlic?" she asked him.

"You can never have too much garlic." She had a little speck of sauce on the corner of her lip. He couldn't take his eyes off of it.

"Could you look through those boxes and see if you can find me a colander?" she asked, turning back to her sauce.

"Like with months on it?"

She laughed. "Handy in the kitchen, Mr. Atkins?"

"Pathetic, Miss Miles."

"A colander. Mine's red plastic. With holes in it. For draining spaghetti."

"Oh, that kind of calendar." He opened a box and looked through it, keeping one eye on her. He shouldn't have come back here. Really. What did he have for a spine, anyway? One of those noodles?

A woman like that could make life complicated without half trying.

But only, he reminded himself, if the romance part developed, the distinctly upsetting stuff. And that didn't have to happen. No, sir. He was going to eat spaghetti, and unload boxes, and then get the hell out of here and never come back. Except to pick up Mac in the morning. And again the morning after that. And again the morning after that.

Life had already turned. You couldn't make it turn back.

He found the colander. "Defective," he told her. "It's missing November."

A stupid thing to say, but she rewarded him by laughing. She laughed again when they heard old Sookie's truck grind by.

"Maybe you should call the police," he said, taking the little sample of garlic bread she handed him. "Of course, he'll most likely have given up and gone home by the time they get here."

"Why? How long does it take them to get here?"

"Depends where they are, but they don't have a station around here, anywhere. I guess it could take an hour or two."

"An hour or two? What about emergencies?"

"What kind of emergency?" he asked. The garlic bread was perfect—crunchy on the edges, soggy with butter in the middle.

"Like a home invasion."

He laughed out right. "I think we did have one of those…1995. Cal Peters got drunk and Mrs. Maude Butterfield found him on her chesterfield in the morning."

"Cal Peters? Any relation to the Peters driving around and around my block?"

"Brothers."

"Does Suckie drink? And wind up in strange houses?"

He decided not to correct her pronunciation. "He drinks some. I think he usually manages to make it to his own house, though."

"I'm reassured," she said, casting him a glance. "I'm serious. What do you do in case of an emergency. Like a house break-in?"

"A house break-in? Robbers?"

She nodded, serious.

He tried not to laugh again. "Half the houses in this town don't have locks. The other half have a loaded shotgun behind the back door."

"Loaded?"

Her eyes were huge, as if she thought she'd moved to a place where she was going to be in mortal danger all the time.

"Coyotes," he said. "Skunks. Rattlesnakes. But no robbers. No robber in his right—"

"Rattlesnakes?" she breathed. "Are you serious?"

He was sorry he'd let that slip.

"What about that kind of emergency?" she demanded, her voice shaky. "When someone gets bitten by a snake kind of emergency?"

"That's a pretty rare occurrence. Rattlesnakes are basically shy creatures that don't like to be bothered."

"But when somebody does bother one of them?" she persisted. "And it bites them? Then what?"

"I guess folks around here grow up knowing they've got to rely on themselves and their neighbors if things go wrong. And they get pretty good at it."

"What about me? I grew up with 9-1-1! I'd be terrible in an emergency. Especially an emergency that involved a snake!"

"Kathleen, are you one of those people who has a tendency to worry? About things that never happen?"

She began to breathe again, smiled faintly. "How could you tell?"

"You got this little wrinkle, right here, between your eyes." He put his forefinger to his own forehead.

She rubbed at her worry wrinkle self-consciously.

"In the unlikely event you have to deal with an emergency, your neighbors will help you out," he told her.

"My neighbors? Like the Peters brothers?" She quit rubbing the worry spot and frowned at him.

What he wanted to say was, *You can call me. Anytime. What are knights for, anyway?* But he was half an hour away, a long, long way if there was a snake in the basement. "You got a nice old couple on your west side here. Retired farmers. Sandersons. And the Watsons."

"Oh."

"If it's a medical emergency, like a snakebite, they bring in the helicopter. Med evac just like *M.A.S.H.*" More late-night programming. "Meanwhile, a little snake sense goes a long way."

"Snake sense," she repeated. She gave the worry wrinkle another little rub.

"Don't be reaching into any dark corners in your basement, especially behind that old furnace."

"My basement? *My* basement? The basement through that door right over there?"

"The noodles are boiling over," he said gently.

She turned to them with a little cry of dismay, and he realized unless he wanted dinner ruined he better wrap up the snake talk.

"Nobody's seen a rattler in town for a while." He didn't add that the last time one had been seen it *was* cuddled up right behind Maude's furnace in her basement. Maybe Maude attracted varmints of various varieties.

*   *   *

Spaghetti was the world's hardest food to eat with dignity, but it made it easier that she didn't have a table set up yet. The weather was unusually hot, so they took their plates out on the porch and sat on the steps. He noticed she rolled her noodles up neatly against her spoon and popped them in her mouth.

Mac was on the other end of the scale, relishing slurping back long tendrils, in between treating him to dark looks of savage dislike.

He tried to be somewhere in the middle. He thought it was probably the best spaghetti he had ever eaten. *Orgasmic.* "This is pretty good," he said.

He offered to help with dishes, but she shooed him away, and he commandeered Mac to help him get the furniture in.

"Amazing how much stuff you can put in one of these," Evan commented on the U-haul, to nobody in particular, since Mac answered him only in grunts. He took off his shirt, ready to work, and tossed it on the hood of his truck.

Sookie drove by again. He nodded at him. Sookie ignored him, as if he had ended up on this block by accident. As if that were possible in Hopkins Gulch.

"Who is that?" Mac said.

"Sookie Peters."

"Is he a weirdo, or something? He keeps driving by here."

"Nah, he's waiting for me to leave so he can move in on your aunt."

"Hah. He might as well not waste his time. Auntie Kathy doesn't go out with people. Not anyone. Not since Howard, the bowwow."

Don't ask, he commanded himself. "Who?"

"Some guy she was going to marry. A long time ago. He's going to marry someone else now."

So, there was a little more to her winding up in Hopkins Gulch than her nephew's welfare. He told himself to leave it. "How long ago?"

"They broke up five years ago. I guess 'cause of me." There was more pain there despite Mac's practiced indifference. "I mean they still went for lunch and stuff 'cause they worked in the same office."

It seemed to Evan five years was a long time to nurse something like that. It did not, he told himself sternly, qualify her as a damsel in distress.

He knew he should leave it there, but who knew if the kid would ever talk to him in full sentences again? He tugged a metal bed frame out of the tangle of boxes and furniture. "Don't you think she gets lonely sometimes?"

"No," Mac said, vehemently. "She doesn't. Old people don't get lonely."

Evan handed him the bed frame, watched to make sure he could handle it and then took a dresser out and started up the walk.

"How old is she?" He didn't think she'd appreciate him asking, but he did anyway.

"She's thirty-four." The boy was panting a bit.

Good. Wear him right out and he'd be less apt to be looking for trouble.

"That's not exactly ready for knitting sweaters on August afternoons," Evan said dryly.

"She does so knit! Well, hooks rugs, same thing. And I'll bet she's a lot older than you!"

"A little older than me." For some reason he liked that picture of her, making rugs.

"Ha. How old are you?"

"Twenty-six." He held open the door for Mac.

"That means when you were in Grade Two she was in Grade Ten. That's a lot older than you."

Evan shot him a look. Mac was getting riled. One more good reason to keep everything neighborly. Which was going to be really, really simple. As long as he never again thought of her lips and his on the same spoon.

"Is this your stuff or hers?" he asked, pausing in the hallway.

"Hers. You were eight when she was sixteen. She could have been your baby-sitter."

"I think I got the point the first time." He hoped she wasn't listening. Next trip, he was going to load the kid down a little heavier. Now that he'd got him talking, he was sorry.

"When she was having her first kiss, you were playing with Tonka trucks."

That big old armchair looked heavy enough to shut him up next trip. Meanwhile they were in her bedroom, and he was thinking of her first kiss, his mind going there despite Jesse, his reminder of kiss consequences, snoring away on her bed. He wondered what it had been like for her, that first kiss. Had it been as sweet and as innocent as pure white lilies coming up at Easter? Had it made her heart pound wildly, and stirred in her longings for things she had never known? He wondered what she kissed like now, now that she had known some of those things?

Was it crazy to be disappointed that he would not be the one to experience firsts with her? Was it crazy to wonder what she would be like in his bed?

Yes.

She was probably mature enough not to even think

such things, he thought, retreating from her bedroom as fast as he could. Those were exactly the kinds of things and the kinds of thoughts that made romance so distinctly upsetting.

When it wasn't being distinctly tantalizing, distinctly world-shaking, distinctly, well, exhilarating.

Sookie was coming around the block again.

Bad timing. Evan stepped out on the road, stopped Sookie, went around to the driver's side of his truck.

"They're starting to think you're a weirdo, Sookie."

"You're just saying that."

"Okay. *I'm* starting to think you're a weirdo. If you drive by here again, I'm going to haul you out of that truck and finish what I started in Grade Eleven."

Sookie took off in a shower of dust and gravel.

"What did you say to him?" Mac asked with reluctant admiration.

"Let's just say I acted my age." He didn't say out loud, young. And stupid. Not in the least like a white knight. He was somebody's dad now. He really needed to try resolving situations with maturity—not by threatening to pound on people. He somehow doubted Kathleen would be impressed with how he had gotten rid of Sookie.

Which was good. The last thing he needed was to be thinking of impressing Kathleen Miles.

His immature mind insisted on adding, *in bed or out.*

Mac grunted under the weight of the armchair. Evan took on the big old sideboard for himself. Maybe Mac wasn't the only one who needed to be worked until he couldn't even think about getting into trouble.

Kathleen looked out the window. Evan had taken off his shirt! Well, why not? He was working hard, and it was unusually hot out, even now with the sun beginning to wallow over that endless prairie horizon.

Why not? Because it could make a woman lose her head. It could make her forget all about her responsibility to a young boy struggling to become a man.

Still, there was no harm in looking. Being on a diet didn't mean you couldn't look at double chocolate brownies with hot fudge icing.

He had her sideboard up on his shoulder, and every muscle he had, and that seemed to be a considerable number, was standing out, hard-edged and rippling.

For all that his muscles were straining, he didn't look as if he was even breathing hard. Not like Mac who was struggling under the weight of her huge old armchair. She thought to protest that Mac had probably done enough today, but the prospect of him just tumbling into bed exhausted instead of wandering around town looking for trouble was too appealing.

Her eyes went back to Evan, the young, raw beauty of his body exerting a magnetic force over her. He adjusted the sideboard, and the muscles in his arms coiled and leaped under flawless skin and fine arm hairs bleached to golden threads by the sun.

His pectoral muscles were deep, and mounded, even his stomach looked hard and muscular. On her way to work, in Vancouver, Kathleen sometimes passed by the glass picture window of a gym, but somehow it was more impressive that Evan looked like this without the benefit of a gym. He undoubtedly possessed this hard, uncompromising man's body because he did hard and uncompromising man's work.

Kathleen, she told herself, how do you know he doesn't go to a gym?

She forced herself out of her trance, and held open

the door for them. He brushed by her. If she reached out, half an inch, she could touch him.

"Do you work out?" she asked him.

He set down the sideboard, turned and gave her a quick, incredulous look. "Yeah," he said. "Every day. From sunup to sundown."

She wanted to touch him. Never once, in all those years of working side by side with Howard had she wanted to touch him. Not even when the engagement was on.

"Where do you want this?"

"Could we try it under the window?" A complete coincidence it was the spot furthest away from them and would give her perhaps a whole additional second or two to admire him while he was unaware.

He lifted the sideboard with seeming ease, moved across the room.

Be still my foolish heart, she ordered herself. He looked like one of those guys on calendars that the women in her office had drooled over. Howard's office. Howard's company.

That ad in the *Vancouver Sun* that had jumped out at her just hours after Howard had announced his engagement and introduced his fiancée around had not said one single word about rattlesnakes. Or the Peters brothers. Or men who looked like calendar boys.

Make that colander boy, she said to herself, watching him wrestle the sideboard into the window well. Mr. November.

Still, his body being at its peak like that reminded her that hers was not. She was a lot closer to forty than twenty. And when men looked at calendars, it wasn't forty-year-olds, they drooled over. Howard's fiancée was twenty-two.

Evan Atkins would probably never see her the way she saw him—as young, earthy, sexy, desirable. A man had not triggered these strange longings in her since, when? Ever?

Even her first kiss had been a disappointment. A sloppy, awkward incident that had left her wiping frantically at her lips.

She had never attracted men like Evan. During high school, she most likely would have qualified as a wallflower—very shy, very unsure of herself. On those rare occasions that she had been asked out, it was always by the kind of boys with wire-rim glasses who wore V-necked sweater vests and belonged to the science club. Once she had started work it had been different. Men seemed to find her attractive, and she had gone through a stage where she had dated a fair bit—but not men like Evan.

Men with business suits, and thinning hair, and little paunchy stomachs. Men who worked on computers or sold insurance or worked with numbers. Men who talked about the stock market, prime and their mission statement. Men who liked improbable movies about men who were not like them saving the world from terrorists. Men who wore highly polished black shoes, golfed on weekends and hired it out if they wanted something heavy moved. Not unattractive men, but not *exciting*. Men exactly like Howard.

That probably, she thought wryly, would explain why she was still a virgin, even after the world's longest engagement, prolonged by her sister's illness.

"Hey, Auntie Kathy, where do you want this chair?"

"I can't believe how strong you are," she said to

Mac, and watched him beam. "Right over there would be great."

The sideboard positioned, Evan stepped back and regarded it thoughtfully. She noticed his skin was now coated in a fine sheen of sweat.

It made her want to touch him more than ever.

The truth was, she had never in her life felt so physically aware of a person as she felt of Evan Atkins. She had never been so aware of how beautifully men were put together, never wanted so badly to run her fingers over silken skin, to feel her softness being gathered in that hardness.

She had the awful, naughty thought that if her first kiss had been with Evan instead of Malcolm Riley, she wouldn't be the world's oldest virgin today!

Of course, at the time she was fending off Malcolm's saliva-filled kisses, Evan would have been what? Ten or eleven?

He's not ten or eleven now, a voice inside her head told her with wicked smugness.

That was the problem with a person on a diet looking at sweet things. First it was a harmless look. And then a little sniff. And then just a wee taste. And then the whole pan gone.

She wasn't sure what that meant in terms of liking to look at Evan Atkins.

He glanced up and saw her. He folded his arms across his naked chest and narrowed his eyes at her.

On second thought, she knew exactly what it meant.

And from the look in his eyes, so did he.

From the look in his eyes he didn't mind looking at her, either. He wasn't seeing her as old, at all. He seemed to be seeing her as something she wasn't.

Daring. Passionate. *Experienced.*

He couldn't really be much further off the mark. He, thankfully, stopped looking at her, and he was giving Mac a hand shoving that armchair up against the wall. Had she imagined that flash in his eyes, a look so smoldering it turned their color to gray smoke?

He glanced, quickly, over his shoulder at her. His muscles rippled through his shoulders and his back as he gave the chair one final push.

She hadn't imagined it.

She felt more prepared to deal with a rattlesnake than this kind of emergency: suddenly realizing she didn't know the first thing about herself.

She longed to touch him. His skin, his muscles, his lips. She hungered to touch him. And her hunger shocked and appalled her.

She practically ran back into the kitchen.

"Auntie Kathy, where do you want the TV?"

"Anywhere," she called. "I don't care."

And it was true. Suddenly she didn't care one whit where the furniture went. Her mind had been commandeered by these strange and powerful longings inside of herself.

She heard Evan say something to Mac; from here his voice a deep and reassuring rumble. The kind of voice a woman could turn to when she was afraid of a snake in her basement or a stranger at her door. A voice that promised sheer and uncompromising strength.

When had she gotten so tired of doing it all on her own, carrying it all by herself?

She heard Mac laugh, reluctantly, at something Evan had said, and felt yet another new doubt crowd her mind.

All these years she had thought and never doubted that she was doing Mac a favor, keeping his world safe from the ups and downs of her having romantic entan-glements. Secretly she had thought Howard would come around. He still had taken her for lunch once a week, seemed to enjoy her company.

But now Mac was twelve. On the verge of becoming a young man.

Who was going to teach him how to do that? Who was going to teach him not to be afraid of snakes? Who was going to teach him he couldn't get what he wanted by sulking or behaving terribly until the other person gave in?

Who was going to show him how to shave, and how to talk to a girl, and how to be strong in the way men were strong? Who was going to teach him how to be capable—the kind of man who could fix a truck, or mend a broken window, or nail the back step down?

Who was going to teach him to be a man of honor? Look at how Howard had behaved! He could never have taught him that. For the very first time, she felt a small niggle of gratitude that he had not come back, changed his mind, begged her to marry him.

Who was going to teach him that the love between a man and a woman was sacred and beautiful and worth any risk and any heartbreak, when she had acted scared to death of it ever since Howard had called off their engagement? When she had played everything in her life so safe?

"We need something to drink, Auntie—" Mac came through the kitchen door, skidded to a halt. "Are you okay?"

"Oh, sure," she said, busying herself at a sink that had already been cleaned.

"You look like you're crying," he said suspiciously.

"No, no. I just got something in my eye."

Chapter Four

Jesse still hadn't woken up when Evan went and carefully picked him up from her bed, tucked him into his shoulder.

"Is he going to sleep tonight?" Kathleen asked, taking his hand, Evan's, and folding his fingers around a container of leftover spaghetti. Did her hand linger on his just a bit longer than was absolutely necessary?

"Are you kidding? It's part of his torture Daddy routine. He falls asleep around four every day, wakes up at eight or nine, raring to go."

"And how long does he go for?" Kathleen asked.

"Until one or two in the morning."

"You get up at five-thirty!"

"If I'm here at five-thirty, I've been up since four-thirty. Don't you see the bags under my eyes?"

"No."

He liked the way she was looking at him. If he was not mistaken, she liked looking at him just fine. And that "no" had come quick enough to make him think she might have been sneaking the odd peek while he was moving her furniture.

"Has he always been a little night owl?" she asked.

"I've only had him since my wife died a couple of months ago. Dee and I had been separated since Jesse was a baby. I didn't see him." He took a deep breath. "Most of the time I didn't even know where he was."

"Why?" she breathed.

"It's a long story. Believe me, you don't have time for it." But it scared him how much he wanted to tell her, to pour out his heart to her. It scared him how much he felt like he could trust her, on the basis of a very short acquaintance.

And one superb spaghetti dinner.

He was supposed to be the knight here, saving her, not looking to be saved.

"Look, would it help if I drove Mac out in the mornings?"

"No. I'll manage." Recognizing he felt vulnerable made him want to push her away, hard.

"How about if I pick him up after work? It's the least I can do. I can't believe the two of you got all this stuff in the house. I can't believe you wore Mac out."

They went into the living room. Mac was fast asleep on the couch.

"You get your boxes unpacked," he told her. "Then if you want to pick him up some afternoons, we'll talk about it."

Jesse muttered something in his sleep, his fist tangled in his daddy's shirt, and then relaxed.

"You're going to have to bite the bullet and get his schedule turned around."

"I think he keeps the same hours his mama kept,"

he said quietly. "Everything takes time. He'll love the spaghetti. Thanks."

It wasn't until he was halfway home, when Mr. Stinky Pants lived up to his name, that he remembered he'd completely forgotten to ask her the most important question.

But it remained unasked for several more days, because Evan was running flat out, torn between the demands of farming and single parenting. He was actually relieved she didn't invite him in again, and not just because he was worried he'd be the most boring of company and go to sleep in his supper.

It was because she made him yearn for all the things he thought he was going to have when he and Dee had said "I do." Made him want to believe again in those very things that had taken his heart and pressed it through a meat grinder.

He'd never had a family to speak of. His ma had died when he was young. His pa was tough as nails and about as tender. Evan had grown up farming this hard country. His childhood memories were of hard work, lousy food, his father silent and unbelievably stern. There were times when he had thought prison might be a step up. Prisoners had a few rights.

He'd mistaken what he found at rodeos and in bars, in fast cars and faster women, for freedom. He'd mistaken excitement for fulfillment.

And somehow when Dee had announced her pregnancy he had thought he was going to have all those things he'd never had: a houseful of warmth and laughter, kids chasing around, home-cooked meals, most of all, someone to love and to love him back. Those were the empty spaces that he had tried to fill in all the wrong places.

He should be older now, and wiser. And way more cynical.

Trying to become a better person—decent, good—didn't mean he had to be stupid. He was smart enough to be wary of anyone who made him want to believe in dreams. And that was Kathleen Miles.

He was dropping Mac off after work, and practically burning out of there. A man could drown in the light that glowed in her dark eyes. Besides, Mac was keeping him filled in on the progress of her other admirers. Sookie had not driven around the block again. Jack Marty had come to call and had been politely turned away.

"Not even lemonade," Mac said with satisfaction.

Mac was turning out to be a good kid. A hard worker, somebody he could trust Jesse with when he had to see to cattle or go out in the field. It occurred to Evan he was really going to miss him when the two weeks were over.

And probably miss catching the odd glimpse of her, too.

"See you tomorrow, Mac," Evan called as the boy got out of his truck.

"Bye, Mac," Jesse called frantically from his car seat in the back. "Bye."

Mac turned around, hesitated. "Do you guys want to come in for a minute? Jesse might like some lemonade. Auntie Kathy makes it from scratch. Not like that powdered stuff you have."

Evan saw Jesse trying frantically to get his own car seat buckle undone. And he saw Mac offering him something fragile.

Regardless of his feelings of wanting to stay away from all the sweet temptations of Kathleen Miles, he'd known from the beginning the boy needed something from him.

"Sure," the white knight said. "Lemonade sounds great."

Kathleen heard the truck turn off, and came around from the side of the house where she was cautiously digging up the garden, one eye ever watchful for lurking snakes.

Mac was jogging up the walk. "Evan and the kid are going to have lemonade with us, okay?" He looked so pleased, took the steps two at a time and moved by Kathleen in a pungent cloud.

Evan was bent over the back seat of his truck, extricating Jesse. He finally did, and set Jesse on the walk, took his hand and they came toward her together.

"Hi, Jesse," she said, gently. "We've met before, but you were asleep. I'm Kathleen."

The little boy tucked his head behind his father's long leg, and peeked out at her warily. His eyes were not his father's, but huge and brown.

"Jeez, is that stinky kid out there?" Mac growled from in the house.

She watched, amazed, as Jesse's face dissolved into a smile. "Mac!" he cried, and squirmed out of his father's grasp. Evan released him and Jesse ran on pudgy legs over to the screen door and pressed his face against it. "Mac?" he called. "Mac?"

Mac came to the door. "Oh, gee," he said. "My first friend come to call on me. The only problem is he's only two feet high."

"Mac play me. Plea?"

Mac opened the door. "All right. You can come see my room only because I don't happen to have anything better to do in this dumpy town."

"Mac, you could always pull another shift at my place if life is too unbearably boring," Evan said. His voice was calm, but there was just a hint of steel in it.

"No, thanks," Mac said. "Come on, Jesse, but listen up. If you make stinky pants, that's it for you. Out. Got it?"

Jesse nodded solemnly and marched in the door. It slapped shut behind him.

"Jesse adores Mac," Evan said.

"I can't imagine why," Kathleen said.

"Sorry. I can't, either."

They both laughed softly.

"I noticed you've progressed from none-of-your-business," she said. "That's great."

"Oh, that's not the half of it. He invited me in for lemonade."

"Seriously?"

"He promised homemade." He smiled, and it was slow and sensuous, a smile that must have turned dozens of women to butter. Dozens. Her own mouth felt a little dry, though, of course, she had no intention of giving in to Evan Atkins's considerable charm. After that night, nearly a week ago now, she knew she had to build a fortress around her own vulnerability when it came to him.

He had a ball cap in his hands and was turning it in circles. Was that an indication he was about to exercise that charm on her?

Maybe he was going to ask her out! A blush crept through her cheeks as if he actually had.

"How was work today, Kathleen?"

She felt disappointed. Really and truly disappointed, as if she had thought he was going to say, "Kathleen, let's go grab a bite to eat together."

Which she should say no to. After the other night
when Evan had been here she had just felt so hopelessly confused, as if she didn't know what was right
or wrong for herself, let alone Mac. She had spent the
whole week reviewing her choices in the past five
years.

She had chosen Mac as her life. Without hesitating,
with never a glance back. What she couldn't believe
was that she had spent five years waiting for Howard—
a man who had resented every day of her sister's illness, and who had been too self-centered to see Mac
for the blessing that he was. Now, she was even beginning to be thankful that Howard's Catholic upbring-
ing had prevented them from ever being intimate together, even if that did make her just about the world's
oldest virgin.

Had it been a mistake to reject romance totally?

It *did* cause too much tumult; it *took* too much. Time
and energy and devotion. Mac needed all she had to
give. When he had first come to live with her he'd been
afraid every time she went out the door, afraid she was
never coming back.

What had been her options in the face of his fear?
Hire a baby-sitter and go on a date? Or rent *Star Wars*
one more time, make popcorn and cuddle on the couch
with the one who needed her most?

Of course, Mac had changed a great deal since he
was seven. He was a confident and independent boy
who would survive if his aunt went for a bite to eat
with his employer. She decided, right then and there,
eating with Evan wouldn't qualify as a date. They'd
already done it once, after all.

But would it be opening the door to romance? And

didn't she need to make a conscious decision about that, not just fall into something?

She reminded herself, sternly, Evan had not asked her for dinner. What had he asked her?

"Work?" he reminded her, amused.

Work. How had he managed to pick the one thing she didn't want to talk about? She sighed and picked a dead marigold stem from her flower box.

"I like the job, but…" She took a deep breath, and said it, "I don't think Ma's happy with me."

"What? That's impossible."

She liked the way he said that. As if he knew she would always do her best, even though he hardly knew her. Still the facts were the facts. "No, it isn't. There's a man poking around. Ma keeps giving me these looks like she's going to burst into tears."

"I'm sure you're misinterpreting it," he said, and came slowly up the stairs. "Pa hasn't been well. She's probably worried about him."

"I hope you're right."

He startled them both by reaching out and putting a gentle finger on the bridge of her nose between her eyes.

"There it goes again."

She laughed. "Did your mom ever tell you your face would freeze like that? When you made faces growing up?"

He took his hand away, and she rubbed furiously at the furrow, until she noticed him looking away in the distance.

"Did I say something?"

He looked back at her. "I didn't have a mom, Kathleen."

"I'm sorry."

"She died when I was just a tyke, not much older than Jesse. I would have liked to have heard that, though. I guess I would have liked to have had a mom."

He actually looked shy, and just a little embarrassed that he'd said it.

"I never used to worry so much," she said, fighting the sudden impulse to touch his cheek tenderly, "but when Mac came along, I felt so responsible."

"I know that one."

"You would. How's Jesse sleeping?"

"I tried to keep him up one day. He won." Evan looked away again, and she got the distinct impression he wanted to ask her something, but he didn't.

"You want to sit out here and have that lemonade?"

"Sure," he said. "You've got a porch swing. I always wanted to sit on one."

"You?"

"Why not me?"

"I don't know. You don't look like the porch-swing type." Which should really be telling her something. Or maybe not. Howard had been the porch-swing type, *exactly.*

"What type do I look like?"

He looked like a man who wouldn't be happy sitting still for long. A man who was strong, and physical and who moved. If you put him behind a desk for a day, he would probably go crazy.

"I don't know," she lied. She went and got the lemonade, and sat down beside him on the swing. It was very close. Her shoulder touched his.

It felt just the way she had known it would when she saw him without his shirt on. Hard. Warm. A shoulder a woman could lean against for a long, long time.

"How did Mac do today?" she asked. Okay. Here was the pathetic truth—she was a tragic spinster, and she liked the feel of his shoulder against hers. And she liked looking at him out the corner of her eye. Just looking. At the little crinkles around his eyes, and the way his muscles in his arms looked when he moved them even a little bit.

"He groused and bellyached, but a little less than yesterday. He's actually a good worker. The funniest thing is how Jesse's taken to him. He seems reluctantly touched by that."

"They're both boys without mothers."

"Mac's got you."

"And Jesse has you."

"He'd trade."

"He would not."

"For lemonade and spaghetti? In a second."

Kathleen and Evan both laughed, but she felt acutely aware of something. Jesse had him. Mac had her. If they ever got together, those boys would have it all.

Got together. Ridiculous to even entertain such a notion. He was the type of man who would date the kinds of women she saw on the covers of magazines—beautiful, not in the least afraid to show off their belly buttons.

And she was the type of woman who didn't date. Shouldn't. Was allergic to romance.

But if she did, wouldn't it be someone like Howard again, a basically boring guy, bald, computer literate, could recite his company's mission statement by heart? She decided she'd rather remain a virgin forever.

"Do you know what a mission statement is?" she asked, by way of a test.

"Say again?"

"A mission statement?"

"No. I mean I could guess, but you'd probably slap me."

She laughed softly. He passed. And what did that mean? That she wasn't going to remain a virgin forever, and that Evan Atkins figured into that equation? Dream on, girl.

"So, you going to tell me? All about mission statements? I hope it's wicked."

"It's not, and no, I'm not going to tell you."

"Kathleen, there's something I've been meaning to ask you."

She could feel her heart beating inside her throat. He was going to ask her out. And she was going to have to decide whether to say yes or no. Two very small words. Why did it feel as if she was standing on a springboard, deciding whether to jump into deep, mysterious and unknown waters, possibly dangerous and shark-infested, or whether to back up to where she had always been safe and comfortable?

She hadn't felt this ridiculously giddy since Mark Morrison had approached her the day before the senior prom.

"Uh, I was wondering—"

"Yes?" she asked breathlessly.

"I was wondering if you happen to know anything about potty-training?"

She stared at him. All right. So this was a pattern in her life. Because Mark Morrison hadn't asked her to the prom, either. He'd asked for her science notes.

"Potty-training?" she sputtered.

"I can't seem to get Jesse to get it. It's the stinky pants issue."

Despite her disappointment that this was about the farthest thing from her fantasy, she laughed. "Evan, you're on your own. Mac came to live with me when he was seven. I'm afraid the hard stuff was already done."

"How did he come to live with you?"

"My sister died. She had a rare form of cancer."

"I'm terribly sorry."

"Me, too. But at least I have Mac. He's very like his mother in many ways. He looks like her. He laughs like her. She goes on."

"Jesse takes after his Mom, too."

"She must have been very beautiful."

A pained look crossed his face. "She was. She was incredibly beautiful."

"Mac said she was in a car accident?"

"Yeah." He scuffed his toe. There was a great deal of pain here, and she had the sense not to probe it. She moved back to the other issue.

"Sorry, I can't help with the toilet training. Is there a library nearby? I'm sure they would have a book—"

"I've got a book. Had a book. I left it somewhere. It wasn't helping anyway. Make potty-training fun. Right."

She laughed again. Why did he make her feel like this? So happy? So alive. In what possible way was potty-training more interesting than mission statements?

It just was. "Maybe that's not such a bad idea, though. You know, I do remember when Violet took Mac off the bottle, she had a little party for him, with balloons and cake and ice cream. She told him they were celebrating that he wasn't a baby anymore. And after, she put away the bottles and the crib, and that was it.''

"That was it?'' Evan said hopefully.

"That was it. We had a great time.''

"I could do that.''

"Yes, you could.''

"Would you come? If I did it?''

"Pardon?''

"If I have a potty party for Jesse. Would you come? You and Mac?''

It wasn't exactly the date she'd been hoping for, and yet somehow it appealed to her even more.

"Of course we'd come.''

"Come where?'' Mac asked, slipping out the door. She noticed Jesse had a tight grip on his hand. In Jesse's other fist was one of the *Star Wars* figurines Mac coveted. "I'm not giving it to him,'' he said defensively, when he saw her looking at it. "I'm just lending it to him.''

"Mac lend Yoda,'' Jesse confirmed solemnly, "to his fwend, Jess.''

"Thanks, Mac,'' Evan said.

"You could show your gratitude by calling it even on the antenna,'' Mac said hopefully.

"Dream on.''

Mac actually grinned.

"I'll invite you to a party, though.''

"A party? What kind of party?'' Mac asked suspiciously.

"A farewell party.''

"Really? For us, I hope.''

"Nope, for Jesse. He's going to say farewell to his diapers and his soother.''

"A pawty for Jesse," Jesse said, wide-eyed. "Pwesents?"

"Oh, sure," Evan said. "Presents. Cake. Ice cream. The works. To celebrate you not being a baby anymore."

"Yeah. I can't be *fwends* with no baby," Mac said.

"Awight," Jesse said.

Kathleen laughed. "When and where?"

"Oh, God. My place. But I have to do something about it first."

"You're not kidding," Mac said under his breath.

"Give me a couple of days."

"That's optimistic," Mac said.

"So, Friday. I'll give you instructions to my place. Maybe you could put away a few party things on my account at the Outpost. And a present. Mac, you want a break from shoveling?"

"Let me guess. I get to clean your house?"

"Easy work. You get to keep your shoes clean."

"Whatever. You're the boss."

Kathleen heard the respect in Mac's tone and marveled at it.

Evan glanced at his watch. "I have to go. Thanks for the lemonade, Kathleen." He picked up Jesse and settled him on his shoulders and went down the walk.

"This idea is stupid, stupider, stupidest," Mac told her, but tolerantly.

"How bad is his house?" Kathleen asked.

"You know, Auntie Kathy, it's a *guy* house."

"I'm not sure that I do know."

"It means you don't wash the dishes until you run out. And everything you eat comes out of the freezer or a can. It means the towels in the bathroom have hand prints on them. And when you drop something on the floor, you don't wipe the spot off. It's great.''

"Oh.''

"That little Jesse is so dumb he didn't know who Yoda was.''

"It's a good thing he had you to show him,'' Kathleen said, deadpan.

"You got that right. Do we have wrapping paper?''

"Wrapping paper?''

"I found those posters I used to have in my room. The dumb Dumbo ones. I might wrap one of them up for the kid. He likes Dumbo things.''

Kathleen found she had the funniest little smile in her heart as she helped Mac wrap up all his old posters for Jesse.

In her spare moments at the store, she sorted through a small collection of toys and picked out a tiny dump truck to give Jesse from herself and a matching cement truck to give him from his dad. She put together a bag of hot dogs and buns and potato chips, and tucked them into the store fridge.

"Where are the balloons?'' she asked a preoccupied Ma Watson.

"Balloons? Right on the top peg above the birthday candles. I used to have them lower, but I don't like putting things in the eye range of children. They bug their parents for them.''

"I think that's actually the strategy of bigger stores,'' Kathleen told her.

For some reason, that seemed to distress Ma even more. "Oh,'' she said. "That's terrible. If they ever do that in my store, I'll—'' She stopped and looked at Kathleen. "Oh, dear,'' she said. "Oh, my dear.''

"Ma, what is the matter? I feel like I'm not working

out for you. If there's something I need to change, please tell me.''

Ma looked as if she was going to say something, and then changed her mind. ''Tell me what you need balloons for,'' she said. ''A party? Is Mac having a birthday?''

''No, not for a while. Evan's going to have a party for his little boy. He invited Mac and me out to his place.''

''Oh, that is wonderful. You and Evan. And Mac, of course. And Jesse. But Jesse's birthday isn't until, let's see, July. No, that's the other Jesse. Jesse Atkins is August.''

''You know everyone's birthdays?'' Kathleen asked, astounded.

''Of course,'' she said proudly. ''You know, people can shop for groceries cheaper in Swift Current or Medicine Hat. They come in here because we know them.''

Kathleen smiled. ''That's exactly why I wanted to move to a small town.''

Ma Watson stared at her, looked down at her feet and then burst into tears. Kathleen looked after her in distress as Ma hurried from the room and firmly closed the door that joined the store to her private apartment.

Ma still hadn't reappeared at closing time, but she had shown Kathleen how to close up and had given her a key, so she did.

She loved the drive to Evan's farm, the landscape so different from the sea and mountainscape of Vancouver. But her uneasiness about the incident with Ma wouldn't leave her.

Evan came out to meet her. ''What's wrong?'' he asked, taking the packages from her.

"What makes you think anything's wrong?"

"That wrinkle is the Grand Canyon at the moment."

Uneasily she related the story to Evan.

She noted that as unhappy as she was feeling about the situation, she still managed to notice how his muscles rippled when he picked up those bags of groceries.

"Jeez, and I thought you hated my farm."

She looked around. White buildings with green trim, miles of rolling country around them.

"I love your farm," she said.

"Okay. So Ma was talking about birthdays, and then she started to cry?"

"Yes. I feel terrible, Evan. I know she's sorry she hired me."

"Kathleen, you are reading this wrong. I think Pa Watson must have taken a turn for the worse. Ma isn't from a generation that talked about how they felt. She's from the stiff upper lip school of thought. It's probably just all too much for her. I bet the doctor told them not to expect another birthday, or something like that."

"I don't think so."

"All right. If it makes you feel better, I'll stop and talk to her when I drop Mac off tomorrow. She's known me all my life. She might tell me what's wrong, but not want to burden a stranger."

"Thanks, Evan."

"No problem. Now lighten up. You'll be like having Eeyore at a birthday party."

"Oh, darn," she said in a slow, deep voice. "My balloons always pop."

They started laughing. Lordy, this man made her laugh, made her feel as if champagne ran through her veins instead of blood.

She looked again at the landscape. It was almost a

moonscape. Gently rolling land, with scrubby grass beginning to grow, but not a tree in sight.

"Do you find it depressing?" he asked.

"The landscape?" she said surprised. "Not at all. I find it quite beautiful in its own way."

"And what way is that?"

"It's like no one has messed with it. It's probably looked pretty much like this since the beginning of time. I bet the Indians rode ponies after buffalo through here."

He told her then, about the centuries old grasslands they were on. "Most of this land has never known a plow. It's grazing land, and not great grazing land at that. A man has to have a lot of acres to feed a few cattle. But I like it. It's big and untamed and I like it."

Inside his house, she understood immediately what Mac meant when he said it was a "guy" house. Though it was obvious that some quick surface cleaning had been done recently, she could tell the state of Evan's house was not high on his priority list. It made her feel the funniest little pang for him and for his little boy. It was as if this house craved softness—someone to care about it, the smells of bread or cookies baking. And that's how Evan seemed, too, as if under all that strength, under all that hard masculinity, he needed something soft.

Mac and Jesse were playing fort in the living room. They had used sofa cushions and bedroom blankets and chairs from the kitchen and had built themselves a tent and a system of tunnels.

It reminded her, poignantly, that Mac was in that funny place somewhere between being a little boy and a big one.

"I wasn't having fun," he told her, crawling out

from under a blanket. "Evan told me I could knock off work a little early if I looked after Mr. Stinky. He likes forts, don't you, Mr. Stinky?"

"Mac, don't call him that!"

"Auntie Kathy, he likes it!"

"I like fowts," Jesse announced. Unfortunately, because he couldn't pronounce his *r*'s very well it came out sounding more like farts than forts, which just cracked Mac up.

Mac made a horrible noise, with his lips against his arm.

"Mac!" Kathleen said.

But Evan touched her arm, and shook his head. She followed his gaze, and saw Jesse was howling with laughter, rolling on the floor holding his sides. She took in the look on Evan's face, and there was such wonder there.

She realized, a little sadly, that for some reason, little Jesse did not laugh often.

"How do you like your hot dog," Evan asked her, "Rare, medium or burned?"

"Medium."

"Damn. That's the hard one." He went outside and she could see him lighting an outdoor fire pit.

Kathleen surreptitiously looked around with interest. She felt puzzled. Was this not where Evan had lived with his wife? If it was, all signs of her were gone.

There was not a picture on the wall, or a feminine touch anywhere.

"Decorations by Zen," Mac said to her in a whisper.

"Mind reader," she said.

He laughed, and ducked back under the tent with Jesse. Their shouts and laughter came out only slightly muffled, and she realized she had not heard Mac laugh that much lately, either. And that she had missed it very, very much. She took a chair and just listened to them laugh and let it wash away the part of her that was worried about Ma Watson.

After a while, she realized Jesse was peeking out at her. After studying her for a long time he came out from under the blanket. He went down the hall and came back a few minutes later. Shyly he handed her a little toy truck, purple where it had paint left on it, two wheels missing.

"This is my twuck," he said. He watched anxiously while she looked at it.

"Pretend to put it in your pocket, Auntie Kathy. He'll really yell about that."

"I don't want him to yell," she said smiling, and handing Jesse back his truck. He accepted it with obvious relief, inspected it and smiled at her. "What a nice truck."

Evan came in, called them to the table.

They ate hot dogs that were only slightly burned. Jesse had to have his mustard squeezed in a squiggle just like Mac's. Mac told horrible jokes, and Jesse squealed with laughter. She laughed just because of Jesse's reaction and because it felt so good to be here, with the boys laughing and Evan smiling indulgently, obviously enjoying his son and her nephew very much.

At the end they had cake and ice cream and Evan put a single candle on the cake.

"Blow it out, Jesse," he called. "Goodbye to diapers."

They all clapped and cheered as Jesse blew out the candle.

Evan relit it. "Goodbye to your pipe!"

Jesse looked a little more uncertain about that one,

but he blew out the candle. He opened his presents, inspecting the new trucks solemnly. But the posters from Mac were what won his heart and made him smile.

"I'll help you put them up tomorrow," Mac told him gruffly.

They all went outside afterward and Jesse threw his soother and a token diaper into the fire pit. Then Mac showed her the calves that had been recently weaned from their mothers and told her that it was one of his jobs to feed them. The calves obviously associated him with food because they came running when he appeared at the fence.

He looked very pleased by that.

It began to get cooler as the sun went down, and Evan suggested Kathleen go back to the house with Jesse. Mac and he would do a few chores. "It'll only take a few minutes."

She did, and was busy doing the dishes, Jesse standing on a chair beside her playing in the suds, when the phone rang. She hesitated and picked it up.

"He's out doing chores—oh, wait, I think I hear him coming. Just a sec. Evan, phone."

He came in through the door, and picked up the phone. She could tell right away something was wrong. He turned his back to her, and his conversation was curt and monosyllabic.

She could hear a growing edge of impatience in his voice.

Finally he said, "Look, I have company right now. Could we have this discussion another time? I beg your pardon? Is it a woman? I think you know it's a woman. She answered the damn phone."

He listened for a minute and then said in a quiet tone

that did not disguise his fury, "You want to know what? She's a hooker all the way from Vancouver. We're having a wild party. I let the dogs clean the plates, and Jesse plays with barbed wire because I'm too mean to buy him toys. Got it?"

He slammed down the phone, kept his back to her for a moment and then turned to her slowly.

"I'm sorry. I lost my temper. I should have never said that."

She stared at him, her mouth open. "A hooker?" she finally whispered. "Me?"

"I just said that because Mac told me you hook rugs. Sorry. It was a lousy thing to say. Sometimes I just start spouting. A fault. One that probably won't make me look very good in court."

"In court? Who was that?"

"Jesse's grandparents, Dee's folks. They phone now and then and accuse me of being a lousy parent. They suspect I don't feed him, or keep him clean because my house is overrun with women and I have wild pot parties."

"Well," she said. "Close. It was a potty party."

He tried to smile, but didn't quite pull it off. "They've requested a home study on me, a preliminary to starting legal action for guardianship of Jesse."

She gasped. "Evan! They can't have a hope."

He shrugged, rolling his shoulders, as if trying to lift a burden off them. She wanted to rub the anxiety away.

"They've talked about this before. I'm not completely blameless. When I first met Dee, I was hardly a parent's vision for their daughter's future. But they don't want to believe I've changed, and I don't have the time nor energy to convince them. Besides, I think if I was okay, they might have to start looking at Dee, and ultimately at themselves. Who wants to do that?''

''Do you have a lawyer?''

''Yeah. She says as long as I keep my nose clean, I should be okay.''

''Should?'' she whispered, wanting to erase the worry line that had appeared on his forehead.

''I'd have a better chance if I were married.''

''That's unfair.''

He smiled, but it was deeply cynical. ''So, who expects life to be fair?''

The phone rang again.

He closed his eyes, and took a deep breath. ''They forgot to tell me they wished it was me instead of their daughter,'' he guessed, and picked up the phone. ''Yeah?''

His tone changed instantly. ''Ma? What?'' He listened, turned his back to her again. ''Yeah, okay,'' he finally said, hanging up the phone. He stood very still for a long time before he turned back to her.

''This has turned into a really lousy party,'' he said. ''That was Ma Watson.''

Kathleen felt dread spreading over her. ''And?''

''She knew you were here. She didn't want you to be alone when you heard.''

''Heard?''

''They sold the store. The deal was finalized a few minutes ago. It wasn't listed or anything. It was a buyer who was interested last year and came back.''

Mac came in, holding Jesse's hand. Jesse's little blue jeans had a dark, wet stain down the front of them. ''I tried to tell you this idea was stupider than stupid,'' Mac said, then looked from her face to Evan's and back again. ''What's the matter?''

"Somebody bought the store," Kathleen told him.

"The store where you work?" Mac asked.

"Yes."

"Does that mean you don't have a job?"

She looked to Evan.

"They want to give you a month's notice. She said you could stay in the house as long as you need to. They'll pay for you to go back to Vancouver."

"Yippee!" Mac howled.

Kathleen turned away. She felt Evan's hand on her shoulder, and looked up at him. She could see the concern in his face.

She tried to smile. He had enough on his plate right now. She said bravely, in her very best Eeyore voice, "I told you my balloons always pop."

Chapter Five

Kathleen swam out of a deep sleep and groped for the phone.

"Hello?" she asked groggily.

"Hi."

"Evan?" She came slowly awake, looked at her clock. It was after two in the morning.

"I'm sorry to wake you. I'm having a little problem."

So was she. That it felt so much like a dream to wake up to the deep timbre of his voice, that she couldn't really be sure if she was awake or sleeping. "What?"

He held the phone away and she could hear Jesse shrieking in the background.

"Oh, my God," she said, coming awake in a flash. "What on earth—"

"Remember the ceremonial torching of the soother? Not such a hot idea, no pun intended."

"He's making that noise about a soother? It sounds like—"

"I know. It sounds like I'm killing him. If I had neighbors the police would be here. I'd be getting hauled out in cuffs. That wouldn't look so good on the court report."

"It takes them two hours to come," she reminded him, marveling at the thread of good humor in his voice, despite the noise in the background.

"That means they would have been here half an hour ago."

"Oh, Evan."

"I'm going to ask you the biggest favor of my life. I'll never ask you for anything else."

"What?"

"Have you got a key to the Outpost? Can I get in there and buy a soother? I didn't want to bother Ma. Pa's sick again, and she sounded about done in herself when I talked to her earlier."

"How could I say no to that? Should I meet you there? Half an hour."

"I bet I can make it in twenty minutes."

"Evan, I have to tell you something."

"That I owe you my life?"

"Besides that."

"You want my firstborn son? Take him."

She liked his voice on the other end of the phone, snuggled deeper under her blanket, let herself savor it. It felt sensual somehow to be talking on the phone in the middle of the night to the best-looking man in Hopkins Gulch. And not at all dangerous, since she would be leaving soon.

"I want you to know," she said firmly, "that you

are going to do just fine if it comes to a court case. I think you're about the world's best daddy.''

She wouldn't have been able to say that to his face, or if she were staying, either, but the phone gave her a strange sense of intimacy that she never wanted to let go of.

Pathetic old maid that she was.

She reminded herself he wouldn't be enjoying this moment quite as much as she was, since he wasn't in bed and since she was competing with a child screaming in his other ear.

There was a long pause on the other end of the line, and then his voice hoarse, he said, ''That's about the nicest thing anyone ever said to me, Kathleen. I'll pick you up. Twenty minutes.''

Twenty minutes was not a fair amount of time to give a woman approaching thirty-five to get ready for anything. She had to be content with running a brush through her hair, scrubbing her face, brushing her teeth. She pulled a button-up sweater shirt and a baggy pair of slacks over the baby doll pajamas she wore to bed and went out into the night.

She was not sure she had ever seen a night so magical—stars in Vancouver competed with all the other lights, got lost somewhere. But here the universe looked enormous, the stars glittering in shining abundance. It made her think thoughts of larger things.

''Is there a plan for me?'' she whispered to the night sky. ''Everything seems to be such a mess.''

She could have sworn a star winked at her, reassuringly. It made her want to memorize the Saskatchewan sky, to hold it in her heart forever, that moment when she felt so sure that, despite all the evidence stacking up to the contrary, everything was going to be all right.

The truck pulled up with a throaty rumble, and she ran lightly down the walk. She could hear Jesse before she had covered half the distance between her house and the truck.

Evan reached over and popped open the door for her, the sound intensifying almost unbearably when he did so.

She climbed in. "I don't know how you stand it. How did you not have an accident on the way here?"

Evan was wearing a jean jacket that fit snugly over the broadness of his shoulders and made him look like a cowboy—compelling, tough, mysterious. Then she noticed his hair was standing up in the front, as if he had run his hand through it once too often, and the cowboy image faded, replaced by one of a young dad, exhausted and frustrated.

No answer. She looked back at Jesse. His face was purple, his arms and legs flailing wildly. She knelt on her seat and reached into the back. She found herself undoing his car seat buckles and gathering him in her arms. "It's going to be okay," she said. "Jesse, we're on our way to the store to get you a soother."

She turned back around, held him tight against her and rocked, talking soothingly, even though there was not a chance he could hear her. At least the flailing stopped. He wrapped a hand in her shirt, and yelled against her breast.

She looked out the truck window at the stars. They were so beautiful. Somehow if felt just right to be sitting next to this gorgeous man in his pickup in the middle of the night. She didn't even mind Jesse's noise, the damp spot growing on her sweater where his tears were falling. Jesse had brought her to this moment, where she could admire the stars. She had not been up at this time of night since she was a teenager.

She felt a boldness she would not have felt in the light of day—as if each of those stars beckoned for her to say what was in her heart. Or maybe it was a boldness brought on by knowing her time her was already ticking away.

And so she said, ''Isn't it a gorgeous night?''

Evan didn't say anything.

''The kind of night,'' she said as softly as Jesse's yelling would allow, ''when a person could believe in all kinds of things they never ever believed in before?''

No answer. Evan put the truck in gear and pulled out.

''The kind of night,'' she continued, ''that could make a person believe in a prince and a glass slipper and a midnight kiss.''

She ducked her head, hardly believing she had said that, mortified. A child was screaming, practically bursting blood veins, and she was trying out as the queen of romance? Romance, something she had sworn off!

When Evan remained coolly silent, she looked at her toes, debated opening the truck door and leaping out to save her dignity. Jesse in her arms stopped her.

Evan nudged her shoulder.

He had his hand outstretched to her. In it were two small cylinders. She took them. Foam. She rolled them around in her free hand, then looked askance at him. He pointed to his ears.

''Can't hear a damn thing,'' he bellowed.

She put the earplugs in, not sure if she was happy to have been saved from herself or not.

Evan got them to the Outpost in five seconds flat.

"Give me the key," he said.

"I'll go in."

"After what I told you about loaded shotguns behind doors in this town? I'll go."

She handed him the key. "The baby things are—"

"I've practically lived in the baby aisle for the last three months. I'll leave a couple of bucks on the counter."

"I'm sure you can be trusted for it." She ran her hand through the sweat-dampened curls on Jesse's head. He was making less noise, sneaking little looks at her.

Evan hopped out of the truck, put the key in the door and was back out within minutes. He couldn't get the soother out of the package fast enough. He turned and plopped it into Jesse's mouth.

The silence was so sudden and blessed that she could hear herself breathing.

Evan leaned his head against the steering wheel. "I knocked something over in there. I hope I didn't wake up Ma."

"You probably would have had a backside full of lead if you had."

Jesse watched her with big eyes, sucking frantically, as if to make up for lost time. Then his eyes closed, opened, and closed again.

"He's going to sleep," Evan said. He tugged the earplugs out of his ears.

She took hers out, too, gazing down at Jesse. He was still sucking frantically, but his eyes were closed and his head nodding against her.

"Look at those stars tonight," Evan said, as if he was seeing them for the first time.

She said nothing.

"It's enough to make a man believe in things bigger than himself."

The silence stretched between them. He made no move to turn on the truck.

"You know how I said I'd never ask you for anything else?" Evan said.

"Yes?"

"I lied."

"And?" she said, amused. "What else are you going to ask me for? If it's disposable diapers, let's do it now, before I go back to sleep."

"It's not that."

"Well?"

He shook his head. "I should go home and get to sleep. I've been up nearly twenty-four hours. I should feel like I'm about to die."

"But you don't?"

"No, ma'am."

"If you call me ma'am again, I'm going to call you—" she thought for a second "—Buster!"

He laughed. "I've been called a little worse than that on the odd occasion. Is that the best you can do in the name-calling department?"

"At this time of night!"

He took a deep breath. Go home, he told himself, think about this. Don't just go blurting it out, and then regret it later.

As if that wasn't the story of his life.

But it felt so magical right now. The stars. The silence. Her beside him, her hair down, a little pajama bow showing at the V of her sweater. His son in her arms, looking so relaxed now and at peace, and the look of unguarded tenderness as she looked at his son made her look like a Madonna.

She smelled good.

He bet he didn't. Which was a good thing. It would keep him on his side of the truck, where he damn well belonged.

"You should wear your hair like that more often," he said. *Back off, Evan.* But it was easy to override that voice when he was so tired. His guard wasn't just down. It was dead.

"Is that what you're going to ask me? To wear my hair like this?"

Say yes. "No." He started the truck. His heart was beating fast. He'd never ever felt like this about this particular task. He'd never cared, particularly, if someone said no before. There were lots of fish, after all.

He contemplated caring so much. Another good reason to make up a question, then drop her off and drive away.

"I want to see you. Just you. No Mac and no Jesse." Maybe it wasn't a question, after all. A statement. His guard dead, and the feelings running free. "I want to see you. Not as Mac's aunt, and not as Jesse's daddy. Am I making any sense?"

"I think so."

"As a man," he said gruffly, "and a woman."

She looked terrified, liked he proposed they jump out of an airplane together with no parachutes.

"I'm way older than you," she said, after a while, looking deliberately away.

"I know you're a bit older than me."

"And I don't date."

"I know that, too."

"Then why are you asking me this?"

"Because I'm dead tired, and the stars are out, and you just saved my life."

"Oh," she said relieved, "because you owe me one."

Say yes. "No," he said.

She turned her eyes to him wide and filled with starlight, her hair hanging in a curtain of silk over her shoulder, her face filled with tenderness and uncertainty.

"Because you're the most beautiful woman I've ever seen."

He couldn't believe that had popped out. She turned rapidly from him. He thought she might be blinking back tears. He leaned over, touched her chin with his finger, forced her to look back at him.

"You are," he said. Sure enough, little diamond tears sparkled at the corners of her eyes.

"You know I'm not. And I don't. Can't. Date."

"Make an exception. I know you won't be here much longer."

"And what will we do with the boys?"

He noted that looking for an excuse was a bit different than an out-and-out no. "Tie them up and feed them to rattlers?" he said hopefully.

"Have you got a Plan B?"

"For the date, or the boys?"

"The boys."

This was looking very hopeful. "Ma Watson?"

She took a deep, shuddering breath, as if she was standing on a high diving board, looking down. "I'll ask her tomorrow."

"Play on her guilt."

"Evan, this isn't the distinctly upsetting part starting is it?"

"I don't think so. I sure as hell hope not. Just two

people who need a break from their kids. When's the last time you had a break from your kid?''

"Not for a while."

"Ask her about tomorrow night."

"All right. You know," she said, "for a woman who doesn't date, I've capitulated with a disgraceful lack of fight."

"Thank God. I'm too tired to arm wrestle you for it tonight. I mean, if I had to I would, but I'm feeling fairly thankful I don't have to."

"You'd arm wrestle me for a date?"

"Best out of three."

"I wouldn't have a chance."

"That's the basic idea."

"Evan." She was suddenly serious, her eyes huge and frightened. "No. I can't. I've changed my mind. I mean I'm too old to be lying awake tonight wondering if I'll have to kiss you good-night after."

"If you kiss me good-night after, it won't be because you have to."

Her mouth fell open. She plunked Jesse in his arms, and wrestled with the door, practically falling out backwards. She hesitated for a moment.

He gave her a slow salute. "See you tomorrow night." She slammed the door and bolted. He put the truck in gear and drove into the night.

There. He'd gone and done it. Weakened by Jesse screaming for three solid hours, nearly out of his mind with it.

But really, he'd thought of nothing else since the moment Ma had called him and told him Kathleen's job was over.

That she was leaving. What would the harm be in

trying to alleviate her anxiety a bit? Get her mind off her troubles, which seemed to be multiplying?

That was all. He was trying on a new role, late in life. Altruism. He'd take her for a nice dinner, out to a movie. Something like that. He was a man aiming for knighthood, after all.

What was this singing inside of him? What was it?

Kathleen looked in the mirror yet again. She had heard his truck pull up, but she was afraid to go out. She was wearing a beautiful white silk tailored shirt and gray slacks, the tenth outfit she had put on.

It made her look old and boring and ready for the office.

She wanted to be able to carry off one of those cute tops that showed the belly button, but those days were over for her. And she'd never even had a baby to blame it on.

There was a loud knock on the door. She made no move to answer it. She had left her hair down, but now, studying herself, she thought it looked awful. As if she was trying to look younger than she was.

Hastily she hung her head upside down, gathered up her hair and straightened. She began shoving pins in.

He knocked again.

With any luck he would go away.

She was just too old for this. The excitement felt as if it was too much. No wonder she had hidden behind her responsibility to Mac all these years.

Mac who had gone to Ma Watson's half an hour ago in a fit of disgust.

Bang. Bang. Bang.

She hastily wiped the bright red lipstick off, then sat on the edge of her bed. She closed her eyes and willed him to go away. When that didn't work, she tried desperately to remember her positive-thinking book. She tried to visualize something positive.

She could picture his beautiful smile, directed at her, full of the most heady tenderness.

"Kathleen?"

She started, opened her eyes and let out a little squeak of shock and dismay. He was standing in her bedroom door, looking at her.

"How did you get in?"

"I opened the door and walked. I thought maybe you didn't hear me knocking. Or were in the basement, dying of snakebite."

She glared at him.

He came and sat down beside her on the bed, too close, his rock-hard thigh touching hers. She scooted away.

"You're sorry you said yes, aren't you?" he asked quietly.

"How did you know?"

He reached up and touched her forehead. "It's running across here in big black letters."

"Are you sorry you asked?"

"No."

"Evan, I just don't know what to do. I don't know what to wear or what to say. I can't even put my lipstick on. I hate this. It's like I don't know who I am, I'm so nervous."

"I'm not so scary."

"Yes, you are!"

"In what way?"

She was stubbornly silent.

"In what way?" he asked again.

"You're very good-looking," she finally said.

He hooted. "And you aren't?"

"Not in the same league. At all."

"That's completely untrue."

"Well, you are very good-looking," she said, stubbornly, as if that was a legitimate thing to hold against him.

"It's not as if I can help it. An accident of birth."

"And you're too young for me."

"Didn't we cover this territory once before?"

She said nothing.

"Can I tell you something?" he said quietly, that stern note running through his voice that she'd heard him use on Mac.

"If you must."

"You aren't exactly acting your age at the moment."

"And what age am I acting? If you say thirteen, I'm going to lock myself in the bathroom."

"How about sixteen?"

"Do you see why this can't work?" she demanded. "You're younger, but you're not acting sixteen."

"You don't know what I'm feeling."

"You are not feeling sixteen."

"Seventeen, then. All scared inside. I don't know what to say, either. I'm worried you'll think I'm a dumb country boy who thinks a bull market is about bulls and stock is about those things that go moo in my backyard."

She smiled, despite herself.

"I'm worried I'll slip up and use the wrong fork at dinner," he said, his hand finding hers, and taking it. "And that you'll think I'm not dressed right."

She let him keep her hand and slid a look at his

pressed jeans, and the nice Western shirt, buttoned high, the shining boots, the neatly combed hair.

"Oh, Evan, you look wonderful, as if you couldn't."

"I'm worried," he said, his voice low, "that I'll order something with garlic in it, and you won't, and then I'll be scared to death to kiss you good-night, even if I can tell you want to."

She laughed a little. She liked him. Maybe that was why she was so scared.

"So can we go now? Now that we've established that we're both scared witless?"

She took a deep breath. "All right. Where are we going?"

"A little place in Medicine Hat. Medium fancy. Can you coach me which fork to use?"

"What makes you think I know?"

He slid her a look. "You know."

"What are we going to talk about?"

"You're going to tell me all about Vancouver. You can tell me about your favorite season and your favorite holiday and your favorite flavor of ice cream."

"That should take five or ten seconds."

"Then you can tell me about what you think you're going to do in a month."

"Another ten seconds. What are you going to talk about?"

"I'll dispel the romantic myth surrounding the rodeo cowboy by sharing the highlights of my brief bull riding career with you. That will be good for another ten seconds."

"You were a rodeo cowboy? A bull rider? Really?"

"Really. Maybe I'll take my ten seconds now." Without releasing her hand, he stood and tugged her up behind him. Talking gently the whole time, describ-

ing a big, wicked Brahma bull with mean red eyes, he
led her to the door, fished her sweater out of her closet,
tucked it around her shoulders and opened the door for
her.

"I do not believe the bull's name was Mr. Stinky
Pants. What do you take me for? A city girl?"

"It was. Well, maybe Mr. Stinky. And he deserved
it, too. Killed maybe three or four cowboys before I
rode him."

"He did not." He held open the truck door for her,
and she climbed in, noting Jesse, too had already been
delivered to Ma.

He went around his side, got in, started the truck and
then patted the seat next to him. Slowly she slid over,
until her shoulder was just about touching his, and her
hip was, too.

"He did. Gored one. Danced on the other. Fell on
one. Other one died of plain fear."

The truck moved forward.

"Thank you," she whispered.

"For what?"

"For making me be more than I am."

"Kathleen Miles, a simple cowboy like me couldn't
do that."

"You're not a simple cowboy, Evan."

"No?"

"I think you're more like a knight."

"Have you been talking to Ma Watson?" he asked
sharply.

"About knights?" she said incredulously. "No."

"I think a knight would know which fork to use,"
he said, recovering, flashing a grin at her.

"Really? I wouldn't have even thought they had
forks back then."

"Good point. Now the rules for this evening."

"Rules?"

"Yup. Absolutely no talk of the boys—not one word."

"All right."

"And no worries. Not a single one."

"All right."

"Now, where was I? Oh, yeah, he had a look of fire in his eye, that bull."

They were nearly halfway to Medicine Hat when he finished the story, a story that managed to tell her quite a lot about the life of a bull rider, for all its tall qualities. It finished with the conclusion that with any luck they'd be eating that old Mr. Stinky for supper tonight.

"Your turn," he said.

"After that? You don't seem to get it, Evan. I'm boring."

"No, you don't seem to get it, Kathleen. You aren't."

"Well, I can't think of one interesting thing to say."

"Start here then—when I was a little girl my favorite thing was…"

"When I was a little girl my favorite thing was going to the Vancouver Aquarium."

"Really? Now there's something I've always wanted to do. Tell me about it."

And it was that easy.

Dinner was wonderful. He was charming and funny and endearingly humble about the very lack of finesse that made him so appealing, so real.

She ordered Caesar salad with prawns on it, and he teased her about the garlic.

"Hello, Evan."

Kathleen looked up. The woman was icily beautiful

in an electric-blue silk suit, the skirt four inches above the knee. Her dark hair extremely and stylishly short, her makeup perfect. Red, red lipstick looked fine on her.

"Mary Anne! Hi. You're not licensed to practice in this province are you?"

"Depends what I'm practicing," she said, sending a look back to her table, where a distinguished-looking man in a suit was sitting. "Law, no."

"Kathleen, this is my lawyer, Mary Anne Grey."

"Hello, Kathleen. Nice to meet you. Look, Evan, I hate to do business when I can't send you a bill, but I got a fax from your in-laws' attorney this afternoon." She shot Kathleen a look, hesitated and looked back at him. Evan nodded that it was okay for her to continue. "They plan to make your life difficult."

"My life has always been moderately difficult," he said.

"They want the court to order a home study."

"I heard."

"You're supposed to tell me when you hear these things!"

"But then it's billable," he said, his tone teasing.

Kathleen watched the lawyer's icy composure give way to her obvious affection for Evan.

"I guess," Evan continued, "I hope if I ignore them, they'll just go away. Look, Kathleen and I made this pact not to talk about anything that was troubling us tonight. Can I call you later in the week?"

The lawyer turned and regarded Kathleen thoughtfully. "Want some advice, cowboy? Absolutely free?"

"Is this a first in the Western world?"

"Probably." She turned back to him.

"All right. Advise away."

"Marry her." She winked at him, and walked away.

Evan studied his plate. Kathleen studied hers. She dared to look up at him. He looked at her.

"As if a lady like you would ever marry a guy like me," he said.

"You mean a knight?" she asked. And then it came out, simply and from her very soul. "I would."

And then she blushed so hard she thought the waiter was going to have to put out the fire on her face. "If I was asked properly," she said, trying for lightness. "Did I tell you about Whistler?"

He shook his head, looking shell-shocked.

"My second favorite place. I love to downhill ski. Do you ski?"

"In Saskatchewan?" he asked, but it was obvious he was thinking of something else, and she knew she had managed to spoil everything.

Chapter Six

Mary Anne and her beau invited them for a drink after dinner. Mary Anne was becoming less inhibited by the second. Evan drank Pepsi and thought Mary Anne's man looked like the kind of guy Kathleen deserved.

White collar. Classy. Rich. He owned some sort of computer company.

He'd probably know how to ask *properly,* a phrase Evan had been mulling over ever since it came off Kathleen's lips.

She had spoken it casually, he reminded himself. For Pete's sake, she had been kidding.

"So, were you affected by Y2K, Evan?" Roger asked, when the conversation slowed to a trickle. "The Big Crash?" It made Evan very sorry they'd agreed to join them.

"I rode a bull named that once," Evan said, drawling deliberately, "and it was a pretty good crash. Busted three ribs."

Mary Anne sighed, took a long pull on her second Irish coffee and said, ''Cowboys are so sexy.''

''Well, not with busted ribs, they're not,'' Evan said. He glanced over at Kathleen, who had ducked her head and was stirring her drink. Had he embarrassed her? Maybe sometimes he was a little too earthy. A flaw.

One of many.

Mary Anne laughed. Roger looked put out.

But Kathleen looked up at him, and the look in her eyes nearly stole his breath away. Whatever she was, it wasn't embarrassed. He thought, again, that she was better looking than Mary Anne—warmer, fuller, richer. He liked the blouse—soft, prim and yet just a little bit clingy.

Roger gulped down his drink. ''Mary Anne and I want to catch the movie, so I guess we'd better move on.''

''Do you want to come?'' Mary Anne asked. ''Evan, you'd love it. Roger's been dying to see it forever.''

''I don't think he'd like it,'' Roger said. ''It's not *The Cowboy Way.*''

''Or *Eight Seconds,*'' Mary Anne said wistfully.

''Uh, Kathleen?'' Evan did not want to go see a movie. At all.

Kathleen was looking at Roger. ''Is it a movie that takes place on an airplane? With terrorists? And then Arnold saves the plane, the president and North America?''

''The space shuttle, actually,'' Roger said with pleasure. ''Sylvester.''

''Maybe another time,'' Kathleen said. ''Thanks.''

Maybe another time, Evan repeated in his head. So much nicer than, hell, no, I don't want to go. These people all spoke the same language.

They finished their drinks after Mary Anne and Roger had left. She'd had hot chocolate and there was a little fleck of whipped cream on her lip.

"I think your lawyer friend liked cowboys," Kathleen said.

"Nah, she didn't. She likes what she thinks cowboys are."

"And what's that?"

"Well, you see a guy for a few seconds riding a few tons of raging beef, and the guy probably looks heroic, instead of just plain stupid. There's something larger than life about riding bulls. It makes the men who do it seem romantic, I guess, brave."

"A bit like a knight from days gone by?"

Evan snorted. "Not hardly."

"Then what is he really?"

"Usually a guy like me. Part-time cowboy, full-time dirt farmer, trying to make payments on a truck, up to the top of his boots in poop of various varieties most of the time. Real cowboys aren't romantic. They're just real."

"Maybe some people would find that romantic."

"Compared to what? A skunk?"

"Compared to, say, Roger."

"Really?" He found this information astounding.

"Yes."

"What was wrong with Roger?"

"Nothing was wrong with him. But I'll bet if he wants his piano moved, he hires someone to do it."

"He looked pretty good to me. Nice suit. His own business. Six-figure income. No wonder he hires someone to move his piano!"

"Evan," she said quietly, "are you trying to match me up with Roger?"

"No! I could just see what the attraction was for Mary Anne."

"Men have no idea what women like, do they?"

"I'll pay you to tell me."

"How much?"

"Ten bucks." He fished it out of his pocket, held it between his fingers.

"Sold."

"So, what do women like? I'm going to write it down and make it into a book."

"Muscles." She plucked the ten out from between his fingers.

He stared at her. "One word is a pretty short book."

She shrugged, flattened the ten on the table and looked at it with pleasure.

"Muscles? You're joking right?"

"Nope."

"It's pretty hard to build a relationship around that."

"Who said anything about a relationship?" she said.

"Ten bucks, and it's not even a relationship. What is it? They like to peek?"

"Yup."

"I've been robbed."

"I'll buy you a drink, cowboy."

"Great. Make it a double. Pepsi. I'm not even going to tell you what men like about women."

"You don't have to. I already know. And it's not their brains."

"Cynic. What made you so cynical? That guy you were going to marry?"

"How do you know about him?"

"Mac mentioned him on one of those rare occasions when he spoke to me."

"And what did he say?'

"That he left you. Because of Mac."

"Oh."

"Is that true?"

She nodded, unable to look at him.

"I don't think you should be ashamed about it. He wasn't worthy of you."

She did look at him, then smiled. "You know something? I must be a slow learner, because I'm just starting to figure that out."

"Did you want to do something else?" he asked. "There might be another movie on."

"Evan, I want to do something that I can't do in Vancouver, that I won't be able to do when I get back there."

"So that's where you'll go?" He felt the disappointment. What did he think? That she would really consider staying here? He doubted that. Even if he asked *properly*. No sense even embarrassing himself by asking. There were limits to chivalry, and marrying the maiden was likely going beyond the boundary.

"I think so. My work experience has all been in big offices. I kind of applied for the job at the Outpost in a moment of whimsy, thinking for once in my life I should be bold and daring and adventurous. It doesn't seem to be panning out. I should go back to what I know, take Mac back to what he knows."

He heard the regret in her voice. "I think being adventurous looks mighty good on you, Kathleen Miles," he told her, and then ducked his head, embarrassed after all. "So, what can we do here that you couldn't do in Vancouver?"

"You know what I want to do? I want to lie in the middle of the prairie and look up at those stars."

He was positive there was nothing in that hot chocolate but chocolate.

"You're not worried about snakes?"

"Of course I am. That's why I'm bringing you."

"I don't think that blouse was made for lying on the prairie, Kathleen. Luckily for you, I keep a blanket in the back of my truck. For emergencies such as this one."

They stopped a few miles outside of Hopkins Gulch and under a star-studded night sky. She put on her sweater and they hiked up to a knoll. He spread out the blanket, and they lay down on it, flat on their backs, but close.

"Do you know the constellations?" she asked him.

"Some. That's Orion."

"Where?"

"See the three stars in his belt?"

"Oh, I do see it."

"And the Big Dipper, and the Little Dipper. The Morning Star. The Milky Way."

He looked over at her. Her eyes were huge and full of wonder. He knew now was the time. He moved his arm over slowly, curled it under her shoulder.

"Is that a snake?" she asked, holding her breath, but her eyes full of laughter.

"Uh-huh. Of the human variety."

He rolled over, and looked at her.

"What are you doing?"

"I like this view better."

"You're looking at me!"

"Exactly."

"Evan, stop it."

"Okay." But he didn't. He leaned toward her. Her

eyes got larger. Her hand moved up and covered her heart.

He brushed his lips against hers, and could feel the tentativeness in her response.

Her lips were sweet, unbearably soft. He closed his eyes, and tasted her, felt her response, and was jolted by the innocence in it.

He opened his eyes, rested on his elbows, and looked at her.

"What?" she whispered.

"You haven't done much of this, have you?"

She looked mortally embarrassed. "I'm thirty-four years old, Evan."

"That's not what I asked you."

It seemed the strangest of ironies. He'd been with women ten years younger who knew ten times more. About what brought pleasure, how to use their bodies and lips and hands.

But nothing had ever made him feel like this.

He wanted her more than he had ever wanted any one of them. And his body was not about to hide that fact.

Probably scare her to death if she knew what was happening to him. He rolled away from her, stared up at the stars.

"Evan, I'm sorry."

"There's nothing for you to be sorry about."

"Could we do that again?" she whispered.

"No," he said, his voice raspy with thwarted need. "No, we can't. I think we'd better go."

He could tell he'd hurt her. That's why she needed a man like Roger, with more finesse, more grace. She needed someone who would know how to kiss her hand, be familiar with knightly protocol.

He dropped her off at her house, but they picked up the boys first, so even though he wanted to kiss her again, felt compelled to taste that sweetness again, he couldn't very well with Mac scowling at him.

"Mac, I'll see you Monday," he said. That should give him a whole day to set things right in his head. To figure out what it was he wanted from Kathleen Miles and what it was she wanted from him.

But by four in the morning when he still hadn't slept a wink, he knew it wasn't going to be that easy to figure out.

Because he was still pondering that *I would. If I was asked properly.*

Asked properly? He couldn't even kiss her properly, a department he had never failed at before. Of course, before, he knew it was going one place, and he couldn't wait to get there. With Kathleen, there was an element of respect there he was not sure he'd ever felt before.

She wasn't a quick tumble.

She was the kind of woman you took to a church, with all your friends and neighbors watching, and said "This is it. Forever. She's the one."

He'd said those words to Dee, of course. In a tacky chapel in Las Vegas, knowing somewhere in his heart it couldn't work, and wanting to desperately for that to be different because of the life she had inside of her. His baby.

Really, it wouldn't make any more sense this time. He'd known Kathleen even less time than he knew Dee.

So why did it feel like he knew her? Really knew her?

He supposed it was because she was more honest than Dee; there was nothing hidden about Kathleen.

From the minute he had first looked into her eyes, he had simply felt he'd known her forever, that his heart could find rest with her.

What had prompted Mary Ann to plant that impossible idea in his head? That he should marry Kathleen?

Well, that's what lawyers did. That's what you paid them for. To make sense of a world you didn't understand.

It would make sense for him and Kathleen to hitch their wagons together. She needed a place to go. There was nothing left for her back in Vancouver. That boy of hers needed a man's influence at this point in his life.

And this boy of his needed a woman's softness. He had seen how Jesse reacted when she gathered him in her arms in the truck yesterday, relaxed against her, trusted her in a way it seemed like he might never trust him.

Damn Dee.

And that was the other thing. You couldn't get any further from Dee Mortimer. Dee had been wild, Kathleen was calm; Dee had been hyper; and Kathleen was steady; Dee had been giddy, Kathleen's good humor ran deep and clear; Dee had appeared strong but had been weak, and Kathleen was exactly the opposite.

It seemed to him that if a man was going to marry, it would make all the sense in the world to pick someone like Kathleen.

If.

Of course, he wasn't going to. Besides, it wasn't as if he needed to get married. He was doing a pretty fair job of raising his son, if you didn't count potty-training.

He realized, suddenly, aghast with himself, he

wanted to marry her, and that desire had very little to do with the well-being of Jesse and Mac.

She was the only woman he'd ever met who would choose the cold, hard ground and looking at the stars over Arnold. Or Sylvester.

She was the only woman he'd ever met who'd been so shy and sweet and uncertain of herself—and yet underneath there flowed a spring of strength and goodness and light and laughter. He could see it in her eyes.

It would be a solution for both of them.

She was only kidding, he reminded himself.

But he made himself think back to her eyes, when she'd said it. They'd skittered away from his—not the look of a woman telling a joke, but the look of a woman terrified, vulnerable. Suddenly he wasn't so sure that she had been kidding.

Which left him right back at square one. How did a man go about asking *properly?*

He groaned, smacked his pillow, threw his covers on the floor.

He wondered if he was ever going to sleep again.

"So what did you guys do?" Mac asked.

"Pardon? What time is it?" Kathleen took her head out from under the pillow. Mac sat on the edge of her bed, glowering at her. She closed her eyes, thinking not of Mac, but of a star-filled night and a kiss that had changed her whole world.

An ember of desire had been glowing within her. That kiss had fanned it.

Wildfire.

And she had asked for more. Her eminent departure from this town had made her into a woman she didn't know. Bold. Brazen.

"It's nine o'clock, Sunday morning. You never sleep in." This was said accusingly.

"I had trouble falling asleep last night. I think it was after four before I finally dozed off."

"Why?"

This also had traces of accusation in it. She wasn't about to tell Mac why. Because the kiss had turned her world on end, and then Evan's baffling rejection had left her feeling wounded and vulnerable. Despite her best efforts it seemed the distinctly upsetting part was going to happen anyway.

How could it? She was leaving. She made herself repeat it three times. Leaving, leaving, leaving.

"I drank hot chocolate. It has caffeine in it. That probably kept me awake."

She had never lied to this boy, ever. Well, maybe once. When she had told him she had made that spaghetti just for him, and been nursing a hope, in the back of her heart, that company was coming. Company in cowboy boots and jeans.

Ridiculous. A woman her age nursing hopes.

Especially about Evan Atkins.

Sexy. Young. Sexy. Strong. Sexy. Gorgeous. Sexy.

Even the lawyer had seen how sexy he was.

"Auntie Kathy, what did you do?"

"We went out for dinner in Medicine Hat."

"What did you eat?"

"I had Caesar salad with prawns."

"You went out for dinner and had *salad?*"

"I'm afraid so."

"What did he have?

"A slab of Mr. Stinky. A bull he rode once."

"Didn't they have hamburgers on that menu?"

"It was a step up from McDonald's."

"Ha. There is no step up from McDonald's. Do you think Evan would show me how to ride bulls?"

"I hope not!" She pulled her pillow back over her face, a hint that she wanted to be left alone.

"Did you kiss him?"

"Mac!" She peeked out from under the pillow, and said sternly, "I don't see how that could be any of your business."

"I'll bet that means you did. Yuck. Did you go to the movie? I just noticed it's playing in Medicine Hat. It's called *Six Minutes to Blast Off*. Sylvester."

"We didn't make it."

"Good. Maybe he'll take Jesse and me."

"Maybe he will, sometime. You know, Mac, I think I'm just going to laze around today. Stay in bed and read a book."

"This book on your end table?" Mac picked it up and squinted at the title. *"A Bride Worth Waiting For?"*

"As a matter of fact, yes."

"Ugh. My teacher says these kinds of books are trash."

"That means your teacher has no respect for women. I'm glad we moved."

"She was a woman!"

"That makes it even worse."

"Is this book about kisses?"

"It's about love and hope. It's uplifting."

"That's all? It sounds kind of boring."

"It's true that not one person will be maimed or killed, and no one will save the world from terrorist threats, but when I'm done reading it, I'll feel happy, and think the world is a nice place to be."

"Oh." Mac set the book down as if he had developed a new allergy. "I think I'll go see if I can catch a snake."

"What?"

"Just a garter snake, Auntie Kathy. They don't bite or anything. Can I keep him in my room?"

"No."

"I think that shows you have no respect for twelve-year-old males."

"My apologies."

"I'll bet kissing is better in that book than it was for real," Mac said, his parting shot.

She waited for the door to close behind him before she muttered, "I'll bet it's not."

She closed her eyes and thought of muscles and all the other things women liked about men. Crooked smiles, smoldering eyes, lips that tasted like raindrops, low, deep voices, an ability to laugh. Sincerity. Humility. Honesty.

It seemed to her she knew quite a bit more about what women liked about men than she had a week ago, or a month ago, or a year ago, or a lifetime ago.

And she knew something else, but did not know how she knew.

She knew Evan Atkins was going to spend the whole day wondering if she'd meant it, when she said, *I would. If I was asked properly.* He was going to wonder that even though he had backed away from her kisses.

She wondered why.

She had seen the look in his eyes, after all.

She decided it might have been the garlic.

She was up, stumbling around in her housecoat, when a knock came on the back door. Evan looking fresh and young and like he'd slept beautifully.

"Come in," she called through the screen.

He did. "Hi."

"Hi."

"Mac called me this morning."

"Mac called you?"

"He asked me if I'd teach him to ride a bull."

"And what did you say?"

"I said I was pretty sure you'd kill me if I said yes."

"That's correct."

"Then he asked me if I'd take him and Jesse to that movie. The one you nixed last night."

"That's a long way to drive to take some kids to a movie."

"You get used to driving."

"Why are you looking at me like that?"

"Like what?" he asked innocently.

"Like you've never seen me before."

"Well, ma'am, I've never seen you in your house-coat before."

"A treat, I'm sure. Don't call me ma'am."

"Kathleen, are you grumpy in the morning, generally?"

"As a matter of fact, yes. How many cowboys does it take to make breakfast?"

"I don't know."

"One, if you slice him thin enough."

"On that friendly note, I'm going to collect those boys and go."

"Evan?"

He turned and looked at her.

"Thanks for last night. I'll have dinner ready when you get back. Roast Stinky. No garlic." Let him contemplate what that meant all day.

"No cowboys, either, I hope."

"I promise."

She spent a wonderful afternoon puttering in the garden and making dinner, not giving one thought to the fact she would never harvest that garden. Evan came in with the boys, who had liked the movie very much.

"How did you like it?"

Evan rolled his eyes.

They ate dinner together, laughing and talking, and then Mac unearthed an old foam football in his room and they headed out to play.

She was coerced into being on Mac's team, and she ran and tackled and ran some more until she was nearly sobbing from exerting herself so much.

She lay down on the grass, and Jesse came and lay beside her, going to sleep.

Evan and Mac continued to run around, until the light faded. Mac declared he was going to have a shower, and Evan joined her on the grass.

"So what's the proper way?" he asked, not looking at her, touching Jesse's curls.

She knew instantly what he meant, and her mouth opened, but not a single sound came out.

"Like would it be with roses, and a ring, and down on one knee?"

"No," she squeaked.

"No?"

"No."

"It doesn't make any sense, in some ways. You know that, don't you?"

"Yes."

"But in others. In terms of the boys it makes sense."

"Very practical," she agreed hollowly.

"And, of course, it would save you a long move."

"Great."

"I'm sure you'd find my place a full-time job."

"Just what every girl dreams of. A full-time job."

"I guess I'm not doing this very good."

The silence stretched between them.

"Kathleen?"

"Yes, Evan?"

"Sometimes I'm so lonely I hurt. I don't think I'm any kind of a prize, but I'm better than I used to be, and I hope to keep improving. I know in Vancouver you're probably used to suave guys like Roger who make about a million bucks a year and could buy you fur coats and diamonds. Do you like fur coats?"

"Not particularly. I don't need diamonds, either."

"What I'm trying to say is that if you want to try this, I promise you I'll care about you and respect you and look after you. I'll treat Mac as if he was my own, and I'll do my best to help you make him into a strong independent man you can be proud of."

Silence.

"Kathleen?"

Silence.

"Are you crying?"

"Yes."

"Yes, you're crying, or yes, you'll marry me?"

Don't say yes, she warned herself. She'd had her brief fling with adventure; she'd thrown her hat in with fate when she'd answered that ad.

And it occurred to her it had brought her right here. To this gorgeous man, who had no idea how good his own heart was, asking her to marry him.

How was that for an unexpected twist on life's highway?

"Well? Yes, you're crying or yes—"

Once you had been bold, it was nearly impossible to go backward. "Both."

And he kissed the tears off her cheeks.

Chapter Seven

"Anyone could have seen Dee was all wrong for him," Ma said, through a mouthful of pins. "Not the kind of girl a boy would take home to his mama. Of course, he didn't have a mama. That was always the problem."

Kathleen stared at herself in the mirror as Ma put another pin in the long white gown. For some reason it was in the store's rather eclectic inventory, and for some reason, it fit Kathleen nearly perfectly. It seemed when there was a plan for you, *everything* fell into place.

Even so, she had tried to reject the dress when she had first seen it, even though her heart cried for it, even though she could not remember when anything had made her as wistful as the idea of wearing that dress.

"Oh," Kathleen had said when Ma had hauled it out. "I don't think that's what we have in mind. We'll probably just go to a justice of the peace somewhere and do it quickly and quietly."

Still, she had reached out and touched the fabric.

"No, you won't," Ma had said sternly. "He run off last time. It don't sit well with folks around here. They'll be wanting to welcome you to the community."

"You mean gawk at me. I feel like a mail-order bride. And Ma, I'm far too old for this dress."

"I think you were a mail-order bride of sorts. I sent you the letter, thinking I knew why, but God knew the real reason. The dress is beautiful on you. Stop this nonsense about your age. Some women age with uncommon grace. I wasn't one of them. Plump all my life, got worse as I got older. But not you."

"Evan has that kind of pull with God?" Kathleen said, trying to joke about it. "I just arrived in Hopkins Gulch, Saskatchewan, because a young cowboy needed to get married?"

"Evan? Evan doesn't *need* to get married. I think it's time for *you* to have some happiness of your own."

"Happiness," Kathleen said, and felt that funny, sick twist to her stomach. "I haven't thought anything through. We don't know each other."

"Kathleen, you are one of those rare people who thinks far too much. You could worry a banana out of its peel. Not even have to touch it, just worry on it. For once, you just acted. Maybe it's a miracle, for Pete's sake."

"But—"

"I don't want any 'buts' out of you. From the minute I saw that boy first look at you, I knew why you'd come here. To love him, plain and simple, and to allow someone to love you."

"Mac loves me," she wailed, "and he's terribly upset."

"Well, that's your own fault for letting him run your life for so long. You're not doing him any favors. That lad needs Evan nearly as much as Evan needs you. But Mac's twelve. Do you expect him to know what's good for him? He'd eat chocolate bars for breakfast if you let him. He's not ready to make some decisions—especially your decisions."

"Ma," she whispered, looking at the beautiful stranger in the mirror, "I'm scared."

The dress made everything seem even more like a fairy tale than it already did. The dress was high-collared, the collar and the entire fitted bodice beaded with tiny mock pearls. There were thirty-eight buttons up the back, making it hug her breasts, her tummy, her hips. Then it dipped in a V at the waist and the small of her back, and flared out in a decadent, ridiculous, wonderful waste of fabric.

Pure white…it was something a young woman full of romantic notions and innocence would wear. It was a dress made for a dream. A dress made for a princess.

Innocence, she had in embarrassing abundance, but romantic notions?

She thought of her husband-to-be, and she could feel her face heat up. All right. Maybe she had just a few romantic notions, too.

No wonder she was frightened. She repeated the sentiment, since Ma was busy tucking and pinning and didn't seem to have heard her the first time.

"I'm scared."

"Good! If you're never scared you're way too comfortable. Real life has some unpredictable moments. It's waiting to give you some gifts. But every now and then you gotta do something that scares you right off your sofa."

"I'm marrying Evan Atkins tomorrow," Kathleen whispered. "Me. He's too young for me, isn't he?"

"Kathleen, you get that knot out of your forehead. It spoils the look of the dress entirely. Entirely. He's not too young for you. That boy was born old. You'll probably lighten him up some."

"What do you mean, he was born old?"

"Darling, his mama died when he was just a tyke, and his papa asked him to be a man long before he was ready. He went through a wild stage—you probably would not believe how wild—but I knew he was just looking for what he never had. What he knew in his heart every person is supposed to have."

"Love," Kathleen guessed, tears in her eyes.

"You love that man, Kathleen, and you will see miracles happen. And if you let him love you back, your life will take on a richness and a hue you never believed possible. You let him be the man he needs to be. He's an old-fashioned man. Lots of guys from around these parts are. He'll want to protect and provide for you. It will be up to you to show him that love, these days, has progressed beyond that. It's about you helping him to be who he was always meant to be, who he really is in his heart and his soul. Personally I've always thought that was a knight of lightness."

Kathleen gazed down at the little woman at her feet and felt as if she was in the presence of great wisdom. It did feel, for an insane moment, as if reality tilted, and that maybe fate or God had brought her here.

She remembered looking at those stars, awestruck, and feeling them answer her humble question.

Is there a plan for me?

But what if this wasn't it?

"I don't know," she admitted, "how much love has to do with any of this, Ma."

"Worry line!" Ma reprimanded her. "Stand still. Two more pins. What do you mean by that?"

"He hasn't. I haven't. Said it. You know."

"Good grief. A word is just a word. It represents the thing, it isn't the thing. I've seen young couples that say 'I love you' every time they draw a breath. I'm not always convinced."

Kathleen forced herself to relax, watched the worry line fade from her forehead and practiced a tentative smile.

She stared at herself, astounded. She looked radiant.

Ma looked at her and smiled. "Now *that* convinces me."

"Are you going to faint?" Sookie Peters asked him.

Evan glared at him, but it was true, he could feel the blood leaving his face, pooling somewhere in the vicinity of his feet. "It's too hot out here," he said, tugging at the stiff white collar that was too tight around his neck.

It was a lie, of course. They were in the shade of the biggest tree in the churchyard. The truth was he was scared out of his mind.

Him, Evan Atkins, who had ridden a bull called Mr. Stinky without his pulse even changing, was so scared he could hardly breathe. Him, Evan Atkins, who had driven cars faster than they were meant to be driven, who had jumped from the peak of a barn roof on a dare, who had challenged his nerves at every available opportunity and walked away laughing, was terrified.

Not that he was about to make a mistake, but that he was unworthy of this woman who had said yes to him. That he didn't have any of the tools to make this thing work. Other people grew up in families. They had some idea how to do it, what the rules were. But for him this was strange country he was venturing into. Like a pioneer setting out in a covered wagon, having no idea what challenges and terrors lay ahead.

He hadn't even told her he loved her.

He felt as if he hadn't known her long enough to say that.

A very good reason not to be making that long walk to the altar in—he consulted his watch—three minutes.

"Sit down," Sookie suggested.

He did, on the grass, heedless of the suit. The suit was not his idea. Black, short jacket, string tie. At least they'd let him have a cowboy hat.

Word had gone through this town like wildfire that he and Kathleen were getting married. She'd told Ma Watson.

Evan, in his need to be a man worthy of her, had dropped by Sookie's and apologized for that day he'd threatened him for driving by Kathleen's house. Somehow, he'd had trouble keeping all his good feelings to himself, and ended up confiding in Sookie he was going to marry her. A mistake.

Sookie Peters and Ma Watson in charge of a wedding. It was like the pair of them had found a bear cub—thought it was real cute at first, but as they kept feeding it, it kept getting bigger and harder to control.

Before Evan had known what was happening, the whole town was getting involved. Preacher booked, church dusted out, hall ready, a decorating committee, for Pete's sake. Presents had been arriving at his house all week. Jesse opened them as they came, looking more and more disgusted at blenders and knife sets, matching bath towels and sheet sets.

Disgusted, Jesse told Evan that wrapped things were supposed to hold toys. Evan had told him what was happening. That Kathleen would be coming to live with them, and in time Jesse might come to think of her as his mother.

Jesse had looked at him blankly. "Mac coming live hew?"

"Yeah."

He'd looked inordinately pleased about that.

"You'll be like brothers," Evan said before he'd thought it through properly. Mac was Kathleen's nephew; that wouldn't make the boys brothers.

But Jesse latched onto the idea with great enthusiasm. He even let Mac, who was still coming to work, in spite of the pre-wedding excitement that held Hopkins Gulch in its grip, or maybe because of it, open some of the presents. Mac was as disgusted as Jesse with the items.

"Initials," Mac said, staring at the white towels. "*EA* on this one *KA* on this one. Yuck."

Evan tried to hide his own horror. White towels? His personal feeling had always been the darker the color of the towel the less handprints showed. Monogrammed to boot. People seemed to have figured out Kathleen was a different class of person than he was.

Jesse and Mac's disgust had intensified this morning when Sookie had showed up with matching suits, and a little pillow for the ring.

Mac was supposed to be an usher; Ma and Sookie were in charge of getting him ready. Evan had been returning his dark gaze steadily all week, letting him know he wasn't going to back down from him, trying to let him know everything would be okay.

He suspected he wasn't very convincing, because he had doubts himself about whether it was going to be okay.

He'd found the two boys hiding in the barn an hour before the wedding and herded them to the house to clean up and sullenly don their suits.

Now the music started to play. Fresh sweat broke out on Evan's brow. The side door of the church opened.

"Evan, get up off that grass," Ma said. "Lord, boy, haven't you ever worn a suit before?"

"No, ma'am." And he never had. In Las Vegas they couldn't care less if you got married in your underwear. He'd been wearing jeans with a rip in the knee if he remembered correctly. He stood up, brushed some dry grass off the seat of his suit.

Ma looked him over and smiled. "It looks real good on you. You cut a rather romantic figure, like an old riverboat gambler. Come on."

Why not look like a gambler, he thought darkly. He was gambling. With his life and hers and two kids thrown in for good measure. He looked wistfully at the open prairie and thought briefly about bolting.

But it would break her heart if he did that, after she'd taken a chance on him, and if there was one thing he was determined not to do, it was hurt Kathleen. Ever.

Meekly he followed Ma into the church. She showed him where to stand at the altar, positioned Sookie at his elbow. He looked down the long aisle at the main door of the church. The church was filled to the rafters, a blur of faces. If he thought it had been hot outside, it was unbearable in here. He found he couldn't even focus on who was there, could not answer the smiles directed at him.

The music seemed to go on forever, and for a sick moment he thought, She's come to her senses. She won't come.

And then the back door opened and Jesse came toddling up the aisle, holding a mutinous Mac's hand with one hand, and the little pillow with the other.

She had said she didn't want a ring, but Evan had bought her one anyway. Not a showy one, because that wouldn't have been right for her. A band of pure solid gold. Now that was Kathleen.

Mac arrived at the altar singing, "Here comes the bride, big fat and wide," under his breath. Evan nudged him and gave him a look. He shut up.

The door opened again, and she came in.

Evan's jaw dropped.

He could not believe that this woman had said yes to him.

She was a princess in her yards and yards of white, the collar high around her beautiful throat, her hair laced with flowers and piled up on top of her head. She looked like she was floating down the aisle toward him, and she looked like all the things he was not—calm and composed to begin with, and sophisticated and worldly to end with.

Her eyes never left him, shining.

Radiant.

No worry line, he was pleased to see.

Maybe she wasn't worried.

She glided to his side, smiled, and her smile stilled the wild beating of his heart. He looked into the calm in her eyes and felt it wash over him. He took a deep breath, and could feel himself fill with confidence.

This was the right thing to do.

Maybe not orthodox, maybe not how the rest of the world did it, but right for him and for her.

His voice suddenly strong and sure, hers like music, they said their vows.

And kissed until Mac, making gagging noises, brought them out of it.

The minister pronounced them man and wife.

"Me got Mommy," Jesse announced, running down the aisle in front of them, apparently having understood more of that conversation a week ago than Evan had guessed.

"Don't expect me to start calling you Daddy," Mac said in a sullen tone to him.

Evan eyed him. "I don't have that expectation, Mac."

Then a flash of disappointment went through Mac's eyes, and Evan had a premonition that this one was going to be hard to win.

Side by side, Evan and Kathleen greeted friends and neighbors. They walked out of the church to thousands of soap bubbles, their guests each having been given a little bottle and a blower.

Somehow he got through it all, the speeches and the food and the dancing that went well into evening, without making a complete ass of himself.

Because all he wanted to do was be with her.

Alone. Away from all these people who meant so well.

Mac and Jesse were going with Ma for a few days, and finally he and his bride were on their way home. Alone.

"Let's stop," she said, "and look at the stars."

So he stopped the truck and they got out, she gathering up her dress, and hiking across the prairie. She tilted her head back, and looked and looked and then looked at him, and smiled.

"Evan, I have something I have to tell you. Maybe I should have told you before. The time just never seemed right."

Oh, God. She was already married to someone else. She was an illegal immigrant and would have to leave the country. She had a deadly illness.

"Hey," she said, pressing her hand against the worry lines on his forehead, "that's my department."

"What do you need to tell me?" His voice sounded grim in his own ears.

The color rose in her cheeks. "I've never done before what you and I are going to do tonight."

For a minute he didn't comprehend what she was saying. "Uh, pardon?"

It was her blush, darkening over the high arc of her cheekbones, that made him get it.

"You've never been with a man before?" he asked quietly.

"It's awful, isn't it? I mean at my age, can you believe—"

"Hush," he said, moving to her swiftly. He looked into the luminous darkness of her eyes, and saw fear and anticipation there. "No one's ever given me a gift like this before. Never. It's the most beautiful thing I could imagine."

He lifted her into his arms, and felt her arms twine around his neck, her head lean against the column of his throat.

He tilted his head up at the stars.

There were never instruction books when a man really needed them, or at least not ones that worked. Not for potty-training, not for this wondrous surprise that had been dropped in his lap.

Step five out of *Potty-Training for the Hopelessly Confused* came to him for some reason. *Pray*.

And then he remembered he had read it incorrectly. It had really said *play*.

And probably both were applicable to the night ahead of them. He kissed the tip of her nose, prayed to be the sensitive guy she needed to get her through this and then felt his heart grow inside his chest, until it felt as if it was two sizes too large, just like a cartoon he'd seen once.

It was like a dream, being in his arms as he carried her across the threshold. He did not set her down, but went quickly through the darkened house, down the hall and into his bedroom, closing the door behind him with a kick of his heel. He set her on her feet gently.

A lamp had been left burning. And the bedroom, too, looked like a dream.

"The bed is beautiful," she stammered, looking everywhere but at him, and the steady look in his eyes. It was an antique four-poster, covered in plump white pillows, the comforter as white as snow.

"A present from the Watsons." He smiled. "The neighbor women have been in here all week, clucking at the mess me and Jesse have managed to make. You've never seen so many feather dusters and mops going."

"I would have done it."

"I don't want to turn you into a cleaning woman, Kathleen. I don't want to feel like I'm stealing your life from you."

She laughed shakily. "Oh, Evan. This is what I

want. To be a mom to Jesse and Mac.'' She whispered. ''To be a wife to you.''

''You know you're a woman who could do anything, don't you? You could be an astronaut or a doctor. And here you are on this little farm in Saskatchewan.''

''Evan, it's not about whether I'm an astronaut, or a doctor or a housewife. It's about me being allowed to choose what I really want without feeling ashamed or as if I have to make excuses. Why do women always have to make excuses about everything, the work they do, the books they read? Right now I've got exactly what I want. Do you understand?''

''Yes, ma'am'' he said, his voice low and throaty.

''This dress,'' she said shakily, ''has thirty-eight buttons on the back of it.''

''Really?'' he breathed. ''Then I guess we better get started. We only have six hours until dawn.''

She laughed, as she knew he had intended, and turned around, her heart hammering in her throat, as his hands found their way to the buttons, big hands, strong, but sure on the delicate workings of those buttons.

''Are you scared?'' he asked in her ear, his hands faltering on the last button.

''No.''

''I am.'' He worked the button free.

She looked at him over her shoulder, then turned slowly to face him, the dress loose now. She waited, her eyes on his face. He licked his lips, hesitated, closed his eyes.

''Evan?'' She could have sworn he was praying.

But when he opened his eyes, the anxiety was gone from his steady gaze, and he looked playful and tender and like the Evan she knew.

He moved close to her, looked into her eyes, his hands moved to her shoulders.

She gasped as the dress fell away, and she was standing before him in the lace and silk of her ivory-colored camisole.

"Undo this tie, Kathleen, before it chokes me."

Shaking now, but not from fear, she did as he asked, taking her time, her hands unsteady on the unfamiliar tie. When it was gone, she hazarded a brief look into his eyes, and then she undid his buttons on his shirt. The buttons seemed as if they were too large for the button holes as she fumbled with them, focused on them, her tongue caught between her teeth.

And then the last one was undone and his shirt hung open. She glanced at his chest, and felt her heart pick up tempo.

"Touch me," he whispered, and her heart moved into double time.

She slipped her hands inside his shirt and touched the skin and muscle she had yearned to feel for so long. Without interrupting her, he peeled off the shirt and dropped it to the floor. She gulped, looking at him.

"Don't stop. Touch me all you want. Until you don't want to anymore."

"That will be never," she said, and then blushed.

But he laughed, low in his throat. "We can only hope."

She could feel a faint tremble in him now, as her hands moved over him, over the broadness of his shoulders, the deepness of his chest, down to the hard muscles of his narrow stomach. His skin felt as she knew it would—heated silk wrapped around solid iron. She reached behind him, and ran her hands down the muscled expanse of his back, pulled herself in close to him, and rested her head on his chest.

She could feel his heart beating. Double time.

''Taste me,'' he whispered.

She looked at him, wide-eyed, and then with a sigh of surrender, she touched her lips to his chest. To the place above his heart. To the hollow of his throat. To his ears.

And finally, to his mouth.

It was the invitation he had waited for, and he gathered her to him, pressed her softness into his hard length and took her mouth with his.

She felt then, the kind of power she held over him, and in his kiss felt his absolute and unconditional surrender to it. She felt the desire on his lips, and saw it turn his eyes to smoke.

She gnawed on the sensuous fullness of his bottom lip, and felt the tremble within him deepen. She nipped lightly, and then his hand made its way to the back of her head, pulled her toward him and he took her lips captive. There was no innocence in him. What was in him was male need—powerful, wild, intoxicating.

He demanded more than little light kisses.

She had lit a match.

And he was tinder. And now fire.

His tongue pierced the hollow of her mouth, and the jolt went down deep inside her to a place she was not aware had existed. He took her lips and commanded, without words, that she give back everything that he gave, that she match him, passion for passion.

Tentatively, uncertainly at first, and then with growing boldness and confidence she met him, explored with him, until she was gasping with pleasure and need so great it bordered on pain.

He tumbled her backwards on the bed. Kissed her toes until she shrieked with tortured delight and swelling anticipation. He rained fire as he carved a path up the curve of her leg with his tongue. And then, slowly, his eyes suddenly on her face, he slid her slip upward and touched his lips to the delicate flesh of her inner thigh.

Then, his eyes turned to molten pewter, his intensity showing in the tautness of every muscle in his body, he slipped his fingers under the strap of her camisole, and paused.

''Yes,'' she whispered.

He slid the silken strap from her shoulder, kissed where it had been.

And then he moved the fabric away from her breastbone, and kissed where it had been. He continued until there were no silken barriers left between her naked skin and his questing lips.

And she did not think she was old. She did not think he was young. She did not think at all. Pure feeling took over, as his lips found the soft mound of her breasts, and he anointed them with his breath and his tongue.

Something wild leaped within her. Wild. Untamed. Primal. As old as the earth. As old as man and woman together.

Her hands slid to the waistband of his trousers, found the button, undid it. Her hands moved to his hips, and slowly, she tugged them off.

His lips claimed hers again, feverish, and she arched against him, begging him with her body to fill her, to fill that part of her that had never been filled.

And then she felt him part her legs, gently, watched as he posed above her on strong arms, trembling from holding himself above her, from holding himself back, but not even seeming to be aware of his own trembling.

"Evan," she called his name across all the time that had separated them in this universe and on this plain of life.

"Evan," she called her welcome to him, as he entered her, filled her, completed her.

"Evan," she called once more, as sensation took her in its mighty grip, shook her, carried her, took her finally, to a place she had never been. To a place where people become as gods, for a few short seconds, where they became heaven and earth, sky and wind and fire, calm and storm.

He lay against her, his head buried in her shoulder, his hair plastered to her skin.

She ran her hands through that hair, nipped his ear with her teeth, then laughed with something that went deeper than pleasure. Joy.

"If I'd have known what I was missing," she finally said huskily, when her breathing had calmed, "I might have tried this sooner."

He lifted his head and looked at her. More than looked. Drank her in, a man who had crossed a desert, dying of thirst, and found life at the fountain of her love.

"If I had known it would be like this with you, I think I would have waited," he said.

And then they cuddled in each other's arms, kissing, exploring, talking, laughing, kissing some more. Dawn was bathing them in its first rosy light when they finally slept in the tangle of their wedding clothes and in the circle of each other's arms.

Chapter Eight

"Darlin', wake up."

Kathleen snuggled deeper under the covers. Then she felt lips on her toes. Her eyes flew open, and she remembered suddenly, deliciously, where she was, who she was—Mrs. Evan Atkins—and what they had spent the night doing.

Evan burrowed under the covers, his head popping out beside hers.

She smiled, looking into the deep, laughter-filled blue of his eyes.

"Good morning, Mrs. Atkins." He kissed her on the cheek.

"Is that supposed to be a step up from ma'am?" she groaned.

"I forgot you're grouchy in the morning. Except it's not morning. We were supposed to leave on our honeymoon three hours ago."

Ma Watson had offered to take the boys for four days so that Evan and Kathleen could slip away to

Cypress Hills, an oasis of earth not far from Medicine Hat that had been missed by the ravaging effects of the glaciers.

"You'll love it there," Evan said, nibbling her ear. "It's exotic, almost like a rain forest in the middle of a desert."

"What you're doing is pretty exotic," she said.

"Innocent. That's called erotic."

And by the time they had finished exploring that, another two hours were gone from their honeymoon.

"I think we better go soon," Evan said, looking at her from one end of the bathtub, mounds of bubbles in between them.

She reached out with her toe and tickled his chin.

"I think we should stay right here."

"What kind of honeymoon is that?"

"I seem to be enjoying it so far," she said. "You know what I'd like to do?"

"Again?" he asked, astounded.

"Besides that. Paint the boys' rooms."

"That sounds romantic."

"You might be surprised."

They spent the rest of the day painting Jesse's room a lovely sky-blue. Evan was a terrible painter, ending up with more paint on him than on the walls.

"Come here," he growled at her, when the last wall was done.

"Are you kidding? I'm not touching you."

He advanced toward her.

"Evan, you're blue!"

"In sickness and in health," he reminded her, moving stealthily toward her, blue-smudged hands reaching.

She dodged. "I don't remember anything about 'in paint.'"

"I do. In sickness and in health, in red or in blue, I swear I will always chase after you." He lunged.

She darted away. He came after her. She ran through the house, shrieking, and right out the back door. He came behind her, breathing down her neck.

She knew he could catch her in an instant. She was not in the same kind of physical condition he was in. He was just enjoying the game, as she was. She felt suddenly awed by the course her life had taken.

When Howard had told her—after their long engagement—she was going to have to pick him or pick Mac, she had been devastated. She felt as if she had invested the best years of her life into her relationship with Howard. They had been engaged for several years, but she had been unable to celebrate a wedding with her sister so ill, needing her, so it had been postponed over and over again.

It occurred to her Evan would have married her anyway.

Hadn't she secretly hoped Howard would insist they marry anyway, that it was the time she most needed support, that he would help her through it, that a large wedding was unnecessary, that it was the vows that mattered and that he would say them to her without fanfare?

But he never had. Looking back, had he actually seemed relieved when the marriage was postponed? And relieved again when she had chosen Mac?

Had he known, somewhere in his heart of hearts, that if they said yes to each other they would miss the opportunity to have exactly what she now had with Evan?

She giggled out loud at the thought, and it slowed her down some.

Because it was really too funny thinking of Howard being passionate. Or playful. What, exactly, had she liked about him?

It had seemed to her he was the most stable of men. Safe.

He was successful at his business, and that had appealed to her, too. In a way her attraction to Howard had been about her own self-esteem, flattered that a man of his stature would even be interested in someone like her.

And in the end, he had not really been safe at all.

As she ran along the well-worn path to the barn, laughter bubbling out of her, it suddenly seemed that that event all those years ago—Howard making her choose—had not been devastating at all, not in light of where it had led her.

That hard choice he had forced her to make had really been a gift from heaven, the very thing that had paved the way to her having the moment she was having now.

She glanced over her shoulder at her husband, still in hot pursuit, then wrenched open the barn door and ran into the cool darkness, up the narrow stairs to the loft, Evan right on her heels.

Finally he took mercy on her and caught her. They tumbled down in loose, sweet-smelling hay, and he put his blue hands all over her until her laughter died in her throat, and she was kissing him with the fever and hunger and passion of a woman making up for lost time.

"I told you you might find painting surprising," she breathed against his neck.

"I love it," he agreed, his lips trailing fire down across her breastbone.

"Tomorrow, Mac's room. Red and black." It came out in gasps.

"I can hardly wait."

"He picked the colors himself."

"I guessed."

"Evan, this isn't even comfortable. I have hay poking into me."

"In sickness and in health, in night and day, in every way *and* in hay."

She laughed. "You're awful."

"Awful good. Say it, or I'll tickle you."

Breathlessly, when his blue hand moved inside her shirt, she said, "Evan, you're awfully good."

He wagged a fiendish eyebrow at her, and then covered her lips with his own. She wrapped her arms around his neck, and somehow couldn't feel that hay poking into her at all anymore, and the last thing on her mind was that her bra had blue handprints all over it.

The next day, while Evan painted Mac's room, Kathleen painted Mickey Mouse and Pluto and Goofy on Jesse's walls.

"Hey, you're good," Evan said, admiring her paintings, but his eyes came back to her and settled there.

She glanced at him, leaning against the door frame, pretty much covered in red and black paint. "Awfully good," she said, and shivered at the look in his eyes. "And don't even think it, until you have that paint off."

"I bet I could have it off in under three minutes."

"You're on," she whispered, and the light that deepened in his eyes made her feel as if she had never lived before.

As if she had slept away her life, until this knight in shining armor, disguised as a humble cowboy, had come along, and literally kissed her awake.

Every day she became a little more certain that she had done exactly the right thing, the only thing. She couldn't touch him enough, look at him enough, be with him enough.

And she knew, beyond a shadow of a doubt, that he felt the same way about her. Evan glowed with happiness.

And then, abruptly, the honeymoon was over. The boys came home.

And it was like sweet torture curbing all the things she felt for Evan, having to wait until no one was looking to run her hand over the curve of a blue-jeaned backside, to kiss him until they both had to come up for air, to hide her burning desire, to haul him down on the rug or the couch or the floor or the grass.

For as much as she practiced perfect decorum, she knew Mac's eyes followed her, bewilderment just beneath the anger.

How dare anyone else make his auntie Kathy so happy?

"I hate my bedroom," Mac announced after his first night in it, pushing his bacon and eggs around on his plate.

"What do you hate about it?" Kathleen asked, helping Jesse up into his chair.

"Red and black are gross. It's manic."

"We'll repaint it," Kathleen told him. Where on earth did Mac get these expressions from? Manic?

"No, we won't," Evan said. "You asked for those

colors, you live with them. Great breakfast, Kathleen. Mac and I will cook it tomorrow. What do you say, Mac?''

"I only know how to make cereal," Mac said sullenly.

"Great," Evan said. "That's Jesse's favorite. Captain Crunch."

"Could you and I talk for a minute?" Kathleen said to Evan.

She stepped out of the kitchen door and onto the small back porch. She took a deep breath. The air was crisp and clean. In the distance she could hear a calf bawling. "He doesn't like his room. Why not repaint it?"

"Kathleen, the room isn't what he doesn't like. You're desperate to make him happy and he knows it. He'll have you repainting that room twice a week."

She knew Evan might be right, but she was not used to having to discuss her decisions with anyone, and she didn't like being called wrong, even when she knew she probably was.

"And isn't it my life?" she said. "I can't paint his room twice a week if that's what I want?"

"No."

She folded her arms over her chest, felt her eyes narrowing. "You're going to presume to tell me what to do?"

"This isn't even about you, Kathleen, it's about him. He thinks this is what he wants, to get us fighting over him. But it isn't really, and if he succeeds, he'll feel so sick inside he won't know what to do with himself. We have to show solidarity."

"Then you should have agreed it was okay to paint the bedroom, or at least to discuss it with me in private!

I didn't like being vetoed in front of him, as if you make all the decisions in this house and I just sit back and say, 'Yes, Evan.'"

Looking at him now, she had trouble matching the man he was now with the one who had chased her around the bedroom until the very walls sang with their laughter. He looked hard and stern, and not in the least likely to back down.

"Look, I'm sorry if you didn't like how I handled it. I'm not exactly accustomed to consulting with people about my decisions, either. I'll try to do better next time, but for now that room is being repainted over my dead body."

She saw the set of his jaw and the look in his eyes, and it made him seem like a complete stranger to her. Which he was, really, if she thought about it.

Which maybe she should have done.

"You're very stubborn," she said uneasily.

"As a mule."

"Me, too."

"Well, as long as we're pulling together, that's fine." He sighed. "Kathleen, if he still hates the bedroom in a month, we'll get some more paint. But he'll have to do it himself."

"I want him to be happy," she wailed.

"There aren't any shortcuts to that! You won't make him happy by painting his room or buying him expensive shoes. I'm not sure that you can make him happy at all, if he's decided that he's not going to be."

"I'm afraid I did the wrong thing," she whispered.

And when she saw the pain flash through his eyes, she knew she could not have said a worse thing to her new husband if she had worked at it.

"I didn't mean that the way it sounded." She touched his arm.

But the damage was done. She could see the hurt in his eyes even though he smiled a little bit. "Our first fight, Kathleen. Not counting the day we met. Maybe we did do the wrong thing if we can't even have words without one of us looking for the exit. Did you think we were never going to disagree about anything?"

"It just seems, after the last few days..." Her voice trailed off.

"What's the expression? The honeymoon is over?"

But she didn't want the honeymoon to be over. She wanted it to last forever, and she wanted them to be a perfect family, with everyone happy all the time. She pictured them playing board games together and laughing while they cooked dinners and the whole house filled with a loving glow, the energy of harmony.

"Aw, don't do that, Kathleen."

"What?"

He pressed her forehead. "Don't worry so much. Just don't expect everything to be perfect without giving it some time. Everybody has a few adjustments to make here." He kissed her on the cheek.

But she knew by "everybody" he meant Mac.

He moved past her, back into the house. "Come on, Mac, let's go do those calves."

"Does my room get painted?" Mac asked, looking between them with satisfaction.

"No," Evan said. "It doesn't."

She came in behind him.

"But I hate it!" Mac was looking at her, his big eyes filling with tears, begging her to help him.

She looked at Evan, squared her shoulders. "If you don't like it in a month, you can repaint it yourself."

"That stinks."

"Speaking of stink, let's get at those calves," Evan said calmly.

Mac threw down his napkin, gave her a dirty look and stomped out of the house after Evan.

Jesse looked up at her, with his big brown eyes, and smiled. "Like paint my woom."

"Thanks, sweetie."

He must have sensed her distress, because he added enthusiastically. "Lots!"

She went and picked him up and hugged him close to her. He hugged her back, and whispered "Mommy" in her ear, a word he could not seem to get enough of, and she wondered how she could have thought, even for a second, that she had made a mistake.

Alone that night, in their bedroom, she could still feel it between her and Evan, a wall up where there had not been one before, a subtle tension. She watched from their bed as he stripped off his shirt, felt a familiar heat rising in her.

"Evan, I didn't mean that. About making a mistake. I just feel so responsible for Mac. I can see he's unhappy and I want to fix it."

The rest of his clothes fell in a pool at his feet, and he slid into bed beside her, scooted over to her and gathered her in his arms. "Have you been worrying about that all day?"

"Yes!"

"You've been doing it on your own with Mac for a long time. I probably should have let you handle it. I guess I just feel men handle things differently, and I don't really think Mac needs the gentle approach right now."

"You think I baby him."

"I didn't say that. It's just that you're so damned anxious not to have a confrontation with him. Confrontations don't break people, Kathleen. He's got to know who is the boss in this house, and that it's not him. He'll be relieved to know it's not him."

"And who is the boss in this house?" she asked, feeling her temper rising again.

"I think both of us can be in charge."

"Is that what you really think, or are you avoiding a confrontation?"

"I can think of other things I'd rather do with you." He reached out and touched her hair. Kissed her neck.

She closed her eyes. It seemed like nothing else mattered but this. Nothing. And she felt guilty for feeling that way, and helpless to feel any other.

And by the next morning she did wonder if she worried too much. Mac and Jesse were in Mac's bedroom howling with laughter, obviously happy, just as she had hoped. When they came out for breakfast the happiness lingered as the pair of them mooed, and made other animal noises through breakfast.

Evan looked at her over his coffee and winked.

On his way out the door, a few minutes after Evan had left, Mac spoiled it all by saying to her, "I know you love him better than me. I know it."

"Mac, that's not true. At all. I feel very strongly for Evan. But it's an entirely different kind of love than what I have for you."

Mac gave her a disgusted look and went out the door.

That night, after supper, she and Evan walked on the prairies; the boys watched TV.

"Mac told me today he wants to go see his dad," Evan said.

"What?"

"That's what he told me."

"Oh, Evan, he doesn't even know his dad. I don't even think he knows his name. The man abandoned my sister as soon as he found out she was pregnant."

Very softly, under his breath, Evan said the word that had recently been removed completely and professionally from the side of his truck. "He made it sound like he knew him. He just had to make a phone call and a ticket would be on the way."

"Why would he do that?"

"Maybe that's what he would like to be true. Anything would be better than me, the one who forces him to move manure. And stole a piece of a heart he's had all to himself for a whole long time."

"He's so jealous," she said, feeling sick and torn.

"Your face will freeze like that," Evan said tenderly, touching her forehead. But when she looked at him, she could see he was feeling distressed, too.

"What can we do?"

"I don't think there's a thing we can do, except be as normal as possible. It would be a mistake to pander to him. I'll just keep working with him every day. He seems to really like farm work. And you just keep lovin' him. You have a talent for that."

"I feel like he's begging me to love him, but when I try, it's like he's got a big glass wall around him that just deflects whatever I send to him. I think the work's better for him than my TLC. It helps him blow off some of his teenage angst."

"You know what I feel really awful about? That Mac is so unhappy, and Jesse is just blossoming."

It was true. Jesse followed her around the house like a little puppy, eagerly climbing onto her lap the moment she sat down, chattering away a mile a minute, loving hugs and kisses and "helping" her with everything. Laundry and making cookies, he had to have his little tasks to do right along side her.

Kathleen even thought she detected changes in the way he said *r*. She read him lots of stories and would have him repeat the *r* words after her.

Still, for all his devotion to her, and hers to him, he resisted surrendering his soother and diapers, and his first loyalty, touchingly, was still to his "bwadda" Mac.

The next morning when Kathleen got up, Mac's room was empty. For a heart-stopping moment she thought he had gone, run away, or in a pathetic search for his father.

Then she saw him outside in the driveway. Right beside Evan's truck.

A feeling of trepidation grew in her.

Evan came up behind her, put his arms around her, nuzzled her neck.

"What's Mac doing?"

At that precise moment Mac stepped back from the truck and revealed his handiwork.

The new word was far worse than the first one had been.

"Oh, Evan," Kathleen breathed when she felt his muscles coil with tension and anger when he saw the word. "I'm so sorry."

"You're sorry? Why on earth would you be sorry? Are you out there with a nail?"

She could hear the barely leashed fury in his words, and then he removed his hands from around her waist, and headed for the door.

"Evan, don't deal with it in anger."

"I don't think it will hurt him to know I'm angry!"

"Please?"

"Don't you trust me at all? What the hell do you think I'm going to do? Beat him with a two-by-four? Is that what you think of me, Kathleen? That I'm just a rough cowboy who can't be trusted to deal with a twelve-year-old?"

"I didn't say that."

"It's right there in your eyes that you want to protect him. *From me.* Have I done something to deserve that?"

"He just seems so mixed up right now, so fragile."

"That looks fragile to you? You know what it looks like to me? Like out-and-out belligerence. He's asking for some guidelines, and I intend to give them to him."

He turned on his heel and went out the door.

She fought back the urge to go with him, to supervise, and instead watched from the window as he talked to Mac. And he was right. He had never, right from the very start, given her any reason to believe that he wouldn't handle it just fine.

As far as she could tell he didn't even raise his voice.

What was happening to her? She felt so torn, as if by choosing happiness for herself with Evan, she had let down her sister in her promise to look after Mac. She had really and truly believed that this union would be the right thing for Mac, too.

Or had she? Had she been pulled by a force within her so strong it would have told her any lie to get her into the heaven of Evan's arms?

And what if the two of them couldn't resolve it? Exactly what had those vows meant to her? At what price to Mac was she prepared to go to keep her promises to Evan?

Both her men came back in the house a few seconds later.

"Mac," she said, "Why? I just don't—"

"Kathleen, leave it," Evan snapped. "I have tons of manure. Probably enough to see him through until his eighteenth birthday."

Mac said nothing, and in fact when he glanced at her she saw the oddest expression on his face. It was as if he wanted to hate this man, and could not. Had specifically thought of the worst thing he could do, had tried to infuriate Evan, like a test. Will you hate me back?

And Evan had just answered him.

No.

The answer Mac most needed to hear.

"I guess I'm going to be moving so much manure," Mac said, "you'll probably have to buy more cows."

"That's right, son." Kathleen detected just the slightest smile in Evan's eyes.

Mac didn't even protest being called son.

Trust him, she told herself. Trust your husband. And then she realized it had been a long, long time since she had to trust anyone but herself. And that when she had stood in front of this whole town and said "I do" she had really vowed to learn all kinds of lessons about loving.

Some of them seemed easier than others.

Chapter Nine

It was Evan's favorite time of day. It hadn't always been, but it was now.

The boys were in bed. Mac had actually sought him out tonight, and they had looked at some maps of the area together. Then, when it was time for Jesse's bedtime story, they had all piled on his bed, including Mac, and laughed at the stories of Robert Munsch. Evan had looked at Kathleen and seen so clearly how happy she was, that this was what she dreamed of, and hoped for. A family not at war.

Which is, of course, what he had dreamed of his entire life, too.

Mac just didn't share the dream. Evan had known it was a momentary truce only when he'd gone into the bathroom after the boys. Mac had written his name on the mirror in toothpaste. Evan wiped it off before Kathleen saw it, knowing how quickly it would erase the storytime serenity from her face.

Now, he and Kathleen had put away the last of the dishes, and the star-studded night beckoned.

He held open the back porch door for her, and watched how she walked with her head tilted back, looking at those stars as if she hadn't seen them last night or the night before that.

When they reached their favorite little knoll, he reached inside his shirt and pulled out a long-stemmed rose.

"Evan! What's this for?"

"Two weeks today."

"Did you have to go all the way to town for it?" She held it to her nose and breathed in.

"Yeah."

"And didn't it scratch you, inside your shirt?"

"Yes, it did."

"Was it worth it?"

"Oh, yes, ma'am. It made you smile. That little knot is all but gone."

She looked swiftly away from him, then. "How can I not worry? Evan, he is being so *bad*. He's never behaved like this. As if scratching that new word on the truck wasn't bad enough! Then the 'accidents' started happening. Letting the calves out, driving your four-wheeler through the new garden, throwing that baseball through the bathroom window—"

"*What?*"

"This afternoon."

"Let me guess, an accident?"

"Didn't you notice?"

"I thought the bathroom window was open." Actually, he'd been completely distracted by the toothpaste, which he decided not to tell her about.

"I just feel so sick, Evan, torn between loyalty and love."

He knew that. Had known it from the first time they'd had words over Mac. He was scared to ask her which of them she felt loyal to and which she loved. They didn't say those words to each other.

It surprised him how much he wanted to hear them from her.

How he woke up every morning and hoped today would be the day Kathleen told him she loved him.

Instead they woke up to some new horror of Mac's and she got that worried look on her face, and the pain in her eyes ripped Evan apart.

He loved her.

He could not believe how it had come to him. How simply this gift had been given to him by the universe.

He watched her with his son, and he could feel the love grow inside his chest.

He came into his house to the smell of cleanliness and fresh cookies and it grew some more.

He watched her plant those flowers, so full of hope, so unrealistic about the challenges of the weather and wind here in Saskatchewan, and the love in him grew.

He went to their bed at night, and she was so full of wonder, so eager, so sexy without having any idea that she was, and his love grew more.

He saw her, after all these years of being on her own, giving her trust to him, slowly, and he took it as a gift he was not always sure he was worthy of.

They walked out here, under these huge mystical skies, and talked, and he came to love the sound of her voice and her quiet insights, her gentleness, her thoughtfulness and his love just kept growing inside him.

As hopeful as those flowers she'd planted.

And maybe, he thought darkly, just as doomed.

How could he love her and keep her when she was feeling ripped up, torn between him and Mac, suffering every single day? This being a decent guy—her knight—was really harder than he had ever believed it could be.

"There's something else," she said.

"Do you have to tell me?" he groaned.

"The Mortimers called this afternoon. They were very nasty. They said they were going to expose our marriage as a sham in court, and that then they would get Jesse for sure."

Forgetting momentarily that he had turned over a new leaf, that he was a gentleman now, he said a word she probably hadn't heard much. She would have seen it though, right there on the side of his truck.

"Evan, would you tell me about Dee? I feel if I understood some things about her I could understand Jesse better. And maybe her parents, too."

He'd never wanted to talk about Dee before, and certainly not to his new wife, but suddenly he realized what Kathleen was offering—not just to understand Jesse better, but to help him heal, too. It reminded him that it was not just Kathleen who had come into this relationship with issues that needed to be dealt with. It was not just Kathleen who needed to learn to trust, to lean on other people. It was him, too.

"I met her at a rodeo. She was a barrel racing queen. Beautiful. Wild. I liked that—that she was as wild as me. She liked life fast. Lots of speed, lots of action. She was unpredictable and unreliable, and at the time, that just added to the whole sense of excitement I felt around her.

''She told me she was protected, so you could have knocked me over with a feather when she announced she was pregnant.'' He tried to erase the bitterness from his voice, but knew he had not succeeded. ''It didn't even bother her to think about getting an abortion.

''I talked her out of it. I thought she'd be as ready and willing to change as I was when that baby came. But I learned a hard lesson about human nature. People tell you right off who they are. And you don't have the chance of a snowball in hell of changing that into what you want it to be.

''She wasn't interested in being nobody's mama. She hated the farm, hated the hard work, and in pretty short order she seemed to hate me.

''Too late, I saw that in the wild no-holds-barred way that she went around a barrel on a horse she simply didn't care if she lived or died. She wanted excitement and lots of it, and there's not too much exciting about farm life in Saskatchewan.''

Or at least, he'd believed that until he met Kathleen. Suddenly with Kathleen, who seemed so calm and so quiet, his farm in Saskatchewan had become a pretty exciting place after all. And that didn't even include the hijinks Mac got up to every day!

''It was like there was something wrong with Dee,'' he continued thoughtfully, giving it words for the first time. ''Hidden behind that reckless grin was the fact she didn't care much about anything but Dee. Everything about her got worse after the baby was born. She was more restless and more angry and more resentful.

''I'd come in off the farm, and sometimes she's just start throwing things at me and screaming. She claimed I loved the baby and not her, and that I wanted her to die of boredom and that I was killing her on purpose.

"One day she took the baby and she left. Took the baby, not because she wanted him, but to hurt me. To punish me for all her shattered expectations, I guess, for me not being able to fill that hole inside her, that I don't think anything could have filled. Really, the more I tried to understand her convoluted thinking, the more I failed.

"I tracked her down, caught up to them once or twice, just long enough to see the satisfaction in her eyes that she was causing me such misery. And then she'd be gone again.

"I thank God every day that Jesse wasn't with her the night she died in the car wreck, one party too many, one trip too fast. I suspect she told Jesse all kinds of rotten things about me, because when he first came he seemed terrified of me, suspicious and silent. He's really coming out of it now."

"That poor baby," Kathleen said. "Both of them, poor babies."

"Dee?" he said incredulously.

"Evan, she never grew up. That's why Jesse is so taken with Mac. That's just what Mac acts like. Affectionate to Jess, but not if it's going to interfere with his plans."

"I'm not sorry she died," he said. "Is that awful?"

"It's human. Evan? I think we need to invite her parents here."

"Get real." He thought dealing with Mac every day was quite enough to ask of a man.

"No, I mean it." Her voice was firm, and he was beginning to recognize when she planned to be mulish. "They lost their daughter, and they're full of anger and rage and want to blame someone, but if you let them come here, they'll see it's not you."

"Yeah, right."

"And they'll see, maybe, that they still have a grandson, and that everything that was best about their daughter goes on in him."

"What if they're the ones who made her like that?"

"I'm not asking you to let them raise Jesse, but to allow them to be a small part of his life. His connection to his mother, and theirs to her."

"I don't want to," he said.

"Just think about it."

"Do I have to?" A true knight would.

"Yes."

And it seemed to him that what he had just said about Dee—that a person let you know right off who they were—applied also to Kathleen.

Right off he had known that she was soft and gentle, but with a core of strength and stubbornness running through her.

Right off he had known in some part of himself that he would be required to be a bigger man than he was if he wanted to keep her—more open, more loving. Yes, even more forgiving. He was going to have to leave that renegade in him behind, the tough guy who could hold a grudge for a long, long time, if he wanted to ever be the man Kathleen thought he was.

"All right," he said gruffly. "I'll call them."

She leaned over and kissed his cheek, and he felt his heart soar as high as those stars up there. Until he remembered one more thing that she had let him know, right off, and that was that her nephew meant the world to her, and that she would always do what she thought was best for him.

And so he wondered, looking at those stars, if being

a bigger man than he was, would involve letting her go, rather than watching her be ripped up like this.

He hoped not. God, he hoped not.

He would give it more time.

Sometimes time solved things that all a man's pushing and shoving and working and fretting could not solve.

She leaned over and kissed him again, on the mouth this time. And before he knew it they were clothed only in darkness, beneath a gorgeous summer sky, and she wasn't even worried about snakes.

In the pleasant afterglow, when he felt ten feet high and bullet proof, he thought about what he could do to repair his relationship with Mac, to get by the boy's anger. He had a brilliant insight. Brilliant. The kid wanted to find his dad. Why not help him? It was something they could work on together, unite them, make it so Mac didn't see him as the enemy who'd stolen his auntie Kathy's love.

Mac gave him an opportunity first thing in the morning. They were working together, feeding the mix to the calves, when Mac started.

"I'm going to find my dad. If we had the Internet I could find him really fast. Of course, out here in the boonies, we don't have the Internet. How come we don't have a computer? How come—"

"Do you know his name?" Evan interrupted.

"Of course I know my dad's name!" Mac said so furiously that Evan suspected he didn't.

"I'll help you find him," Evan said.

Mac froze, and Evan suddenly wished that he had discussed this with Kathleen, because the look on Mac's face was not one of undying gratitude.

He looked very young and very vulnerable.

And he looked terrified.

He turned swiftly away from Evan's probing gaze. "That would be great," he said. "We'll find my dad and I'll go live with him."

"Whoa, buddy. Nobody said anything about that. I'll help you find him and then we'll talk to your auntie Kathleen about what to do next. Maybe you could write him some letters or something, arrange to meet him later."

Mac didn't say anything.

"Next week, okay? After Jesse's grandparents come on Sunday."

"I can't wait," Mac said, but Evan heard something else, and wished he wouldn't have opened his mouth.

Kathleen looked at the flowers in the vase. Scraggly, her bedding plants were not holding out very well against the ravages of the wind. Still, there had been a few blossoms to pick, and with the long-lasting rose Evan had given her, it looked quite nice.

She glanced at the clock. The Mortimers should be here within the hour.

Evan came in and smiled at her flowers.

"Are they pathetic?" she asked.

"They're pretty."

"Could you go get the boys? Mac took Jesse out to the barn to play with the new kittens. I haven't seen them for a while. Jesse will need a bath."

"The Mortimers sounded so excited to be coming, Kathleen. I think you were right."

"I'll try not to rub it in."

"Very gracious of you."

She wanted to tell him right now. That she loved him. When she got up in the morning the words went through her head, and they went though it all day long. In light of the rather intimate things they were doing, why did the words seem so scary to say?

Maybe it was because Mac was behaving so badly. How long could Evan stand it? How long before he suggested maybe this wasn't working? And what did that say about her? That she was attaching a condition to her love? That he had to keep her in order for her to love him?

Keep her, she thought, as if he could return her to the store and get a new one or something. He would never break those vows he had said. Never. Was it going to be up to her to let him out of this?

"Now what are you worried about?" he said, pressing the line on her forehead.

"I think I'm wrecking your life," she whispered.

"Wrecking my life?"

"If you've had enough of Mac destroying your property, I'll understand."

"Maybe what you're trying to say is that you've had enough of the tension between us," he said softly.

Was he giving her a way out? But the thought of leaving him filled her with such an ache she thought she would cry. She was not even sure she could do that for Mac. What kind of person had she become? Only able to think about herself? Was what she felt for Evan really love if it made her self-centered instead of a better person?

"We'll talk later," she said. "Please, go get the boys."

With one more shrewd look at her, he went out the back door. But when he returned, nearly half an hour later, he looked pale and distraught. "I've looked everywhere, Kathleen. I can't find them."

She stared at him. "You can't find them? But that's impossible. Where would they go?"

They searched the farm together, and then the house. Mac's note was in his room, laying on his pillow.

Poorly spelled and stained with tears, Kathleen picked it up and read it out loud.

Dear Aunt Kathy:

I have been very bad and I'm sorry. I see you are very happy, except for me, and I know you don't want me anymore. Old bowwow already left because of me, and pretty soon Evan will, too. I don't make anybody happy, just mad and sad. I don't know why. I guess I feel mad and sad all the time. My mom died, and my dad never wanted me, and I wonder if it's my fault those things happened, and no wonder nobody wants me around.

Evan said he would help me find my dad. That means he wants to get rid of me, too.

"God," Evan said.

"What's this about his dad?"

"Aw, Kathleen, I thought if I offered to help him with that he wouldn't be so angry with me, wouldn't feel we were on opposite teams. It was a dumb mistake."

"It was a nice thing to do," she said sternly, and then continued to read the letter out loud:

Jesse really likes me, and I like him, too, even if he is a real Stinky Pants. But he has a real dad, and now he calls you Mom, and his real grandma and grandpa are coming to see him. I don't have a grandma and grandpa and nobody will ever

come see me. Someday I bet he'll have a real
brother or sister. And I won't have that, ever.

Don't worry about me. I am going back to Vancouver. It is warm there and people can live on
the streets even in the winter. I can be a squeegee
kid just like those ones you always give money
to. Don't come looking because I have a secret
route planned and you will never find me.

Bye forever. I love you. Mac

P.S. Jesse is in the barn playing with the kittens.
I told him not to come with me. You know he
listens to me.

"Oh, my God," Kathleen said. She sank into a chair
and held the letter, read it again, the tears spilling down
her face. "Where could he have gone? And where is
Jesse?"

Evan's face looked taut and pained. "I think he decided not to listen to Mac this time."

She looked at Evan, stricken. "Where do you think
he would go? He's got to be our first concern. He's
smaller."

"I think he's following Mac, wherever Mac is. The
question is, does Mac know yet? How long has he been
gone?"

She looked at the clock in distress. "At least an
hour, closer to two. Why didn't I check on them?"

"You are not to blame. Why would you check on
them? They've played in the barn before for hours. I'm
going to go saddle a horse. This note is making me
wonder if he decided to try to cross-country to the
highway. He was asking me about that a few days ago,
when I was showing him a map."

"You are not to blame, either."

"Maybe I am, Kathleen. I could see how unhappy that boy was, and how unhappy he was making you."

"It's you he was making unhappy," she said.

"Me? I could handle ten kids just like him with one arm tied behind my back just to be with you. Look, I want you to call the police. And then Ma Watson. Tell her what happened and tell her to get the word out that we need as many people as possible to come out here. They can bring horses or be prepared to search on foot, but no all-terrain vehicles. It's going to get dark, and I don't want anybody running over those kids. After you've called, hop in the truck and drive toward town. Look in the ditches, and go slow by anything they might be hiding behind."

She registered every word he said, but somehow her mind stopped on *just to be with you,* and those words in all their quiet simplicity kept the panic at bay and made her feel stronger than she had ever felt.

"What if all those people come and Mac and Jesse are asleep under a pile of hay?"

"I can't take that chance. The people in this country would rather be called on to help too soon than be on the receiving end of bad news too late."

They heard a car pull up outside the house. Evan looked baffled and then he scowled.

"The Mortimers," he said. "Perfect bloody timing."

"It is perfect timing," she said. "Because I'm going to put them in charge of the command center, and I'm going with you. Saddle two horses."

"Have you ever ridden before?"

"Yes." She didn't tell him it had been a Shetland

pony that went around in a circle at the fair. "Go get the horses ready."

And while he went out the back door, she went to the front.

Briefly she introduced herself, told them what had happened and what she needed done, and was impressed with Ron Mortimer's immediate take-charge attitude.

In no time he was set up at the kitchen table with Evan's address book and photographs of both the boys. After he had hung up from Ma Watson, he asked her the names of the local radio stations.

Fiona Mortimer asked her where her coffeepot was, and supplies to make sandwiches. "We'll need to feed those searchers if the boys aren't found right away."

"Thank you," Kathleen said. "I'm so sorry. I can't imagine the shock this is for you. I have to go—"

"You wait five minutes. Go find warm clothes for you and Evan. And when you come back I'll have sandwiches ready for you. Where's your thermos?"

With that Fiona hustled Kathleen out of the room. In a few minutes, Kathleen was running toward the barn, full thermoses, warm clothes and sandwiches with her.

Evan had two horses ready. They looked huge to her, but she would not allow herself to be timid. Not now. Not with that knowledge tucked inside her that he would do anything to be with her.

He helped her mount, watched critically as she got on. Grimly he said, "I suppose they're in there talking about custody now for sure."

"Evan," she said, "I think you might be surprised."

He swung on his horse, the Mortimers already dismissed from his mind.

''I want to go this way,'' he said, pointing. ''I found a partial print on the ground, and Mac asked all kinds of questions when we looked at that map together. You could eventually join the highway, cross-country, if you went this way. But it's thirty miles of rugged going. A map doesn't show the river coulees between here and there.''

Kathleen looked at the prairie and felt overwhelmed by how huge it was. If they went a few steps different than the boys, how were they going to find them? Were the boys even together? She drew in a long, shuddering breath, told herself to be strong.

She suddenly came face-to-face with a fact she had not acknowledged in her entire life. Worrying would solve nothing. Only action would.

And Evan was a man of action.

Chapter Ten

"They've been this way."

Kathleen sat in her saddle, aching with weariness. She looked at Evan, crouched down in front of his horse peering at the ground. Never before had she so appreciated the toughness at his very core. She knew he would not quit until he found their boys.

"What have you found?" she asked. At first she had gotten on and off her horse every time he did, but she had soon found out it was much harder than it looked, and that she needed to conserve her energy.

When she thought she could just weep because she was so frightened for Mac and Jesse, and her muscles ached from the unfamiliar motion of riding, she would think of Jesse's sturdy little legs and wonder how on earth he had walked this far.

Evan had found tracks that suggested both the boys had come this way.

For the first time she'd been very pleased about those expensive runners she had bought for Mac. They left a distinctive name brand anyplace the soil was bare and damp.

"I think this is Jesse. I think he sat down here, from the size of the patch of grass that is flattened." He squinted closer. "It looks like he scuffed around in the dirt with his truck a little bit."

She closed her eyes, seeing Jesse sitting in the grass, singing to himself, tired, playing with his truck. Did he still have Mac in his sights? Was he scared or was he too innocent to know that he had anything to be scared about?

Tracking the boys took an enormous amount of time and patience. Evan rode in a slow serpentine, so as not to miss anything, got off his horse often to look at the ground, at the way grass was flattened, at scuffs in mud—most of which had nothing to do with the boys.

He would also stop his horse frequently, silently scanning the horizon. Seeing him this way, sitting his horse, it was as if Kathleen was seeing what and who Evan really was. Straight-backed, proud, strong, capable, able to take on a rugged, rugged world, and be a victor over its challenges. She was so glad it was Evan looking for these boys. She could not think of one other person on the face of the earth she would have wanted, or trusted, with this task.

She, too, scanned the endless rolling landscape, looking so hard it felt like her eyes were watering all the time, like she was seeing things that were not there.

"Get off your horse for a minute, Kathleen. Stretch your legs. We'll have some of that coffee."

"I can keep going," she said stubbornly. She didn't want him making concessions to her weaknesses that might cost them valuable minutes in their search.

"If we don't look after ourselves, if we start getting

too hungry or too tired or too sore, we won't be as alert as we need to be. We might miss something.''

She got off the horse, thinking maybe that was true of everything in life. That a person had to learn to care for themselves first, before they were any good to anyone else.

''Maybe,'' she said out loud, getting off the horse, hearing her knees crack as her feet touched the ground, ''that's the mistake I made with Mac. I always put him first. When I stopped—'' Her voice choked.

Evan poured a cup of coffee from the thermos, and held it to her lips. She took a deep, shuddering sip of it.

''I don't want you talking like that. As if it's your fault. If anyone's to blame, it's me, trying to play hero, offering to help him find his dad. I thought he would see it for what it was—me trying to tell him how much I cared about him. Instead he thought I was trying to get rid of him. I guess that's what happens when a guy like me tries to be a hero.''

''What do you mean, a guy like you?''

''Kathleen, I've lived pretty close to the edge most of my life. I've been wild and irresponsible and about as devil-may-care as they come. I've looked after myself, and I never got good at seeing another person's point of view. Even with Dee, I could never see what she wanted, only what I wanted. And then when you came along, I thought you deserved something better.'' He laughed, a harsh, self-depreciating sound. ''I thought I could make myself into a knight for you. Maybe Mac could see through all that.''

''You listen to me, Evan,'' she said, her voice low and full of fury. ''I won't listen to you talk about yourself like that. I won't. I've watched you with your son and my nephew, I've seen—'' she blushed thinking of their wedding night ''—the great and uncommon tenderness you are capable of. And yet, when you are called on to be strong and sure, to remain calm in a crisis, you can do that, too. If you are not a knight, then there is no such thing. And if there is no such thing, my heart will be broken.

''I have searched all my life for what I see in you—integrity, strength and tenderness. I looked in those men who are so suave and so sophisticated, who knew what to wear and what fork to use and what wine to order. Not one of those men would be worthy to hold your horse for you, Evan. Not one of them. There is not one man on this earth who I would want here with me more than you.''

''You wouldn't be in this predicament right now if it weren't for me.''

''Really? It seems to me Mac has been a predicament looking for a place to happen for sometime. This was my meaning—that no matter what kind of distress I ever found myself in, it would always be your name I would call. Maybe you don't have a suit of shining armor, but you're real, Evan. You aren't trying to be something you are not, you are trying to uncover what you really are. I knew what you really were from the first moment I looked into your eyes. And I knew you would help me become what I really am, too. That's why I love you. That's why I have loved you from almost the first moment I laid eyes on you.''

He was smiling, a slow, sweet smile that nearly melted her heart.

''You just like the way I fill out a pair of blue jeans,'' he said.

And she smiled back at him. "I'd take blue jeans over armor any day."

And then, as if they had needed a break from the terrible tension they were under, they held each other, and laughed. She laughed until the laughter became tears, and she sobbed helplessly against him as she listened to him say, over and over, that he loved her. That he planned to love her forever. No matter what.

"What do you mean, no matter what?" she asked, stepping back from him, mopping the tears from her eyes with her shirtsleeve.

"I mean if you decide that you have to leave me to give Mac the life you want to give him, I will still love you. I'll wait for you. I promise."

She thought how very different that was than what Howard had said all those years ago.

"That's funny," she said. "I was waiting to say the exact same thing to you, only reversed. That if you couldn't handle Mac anymore, and all the terrible things he does, then I would go."

"Ma'am, I already told you I could handle ten more just like him. Just to be with you. But here's another truth. I love that kid. He's so much like I was at that age it's spooky. That's what I needed to tell him the other day. Not that I would help him find his dad, but that I wanted more than anything on earth to be his dad."

She suddenly had a sense of something relaxing within her, the tension leaving, a river of peace taking its place. Everything was part of the plan. Everything.

Mac had brought her and Evan together, and now he had been the one who had allowed them to finally express their true feelings for each other.

She knew they would find him, and that this moment, searching the prairies, would become the pivotal one in the family history that was just beginning.

That moment when truth made itself known to them.

The simplest of truths, the strongest of truths, the only truth.

Love was everything.

Without it a man could wander forever in his own uncertainties. With it people became strong, discovered who they were and how they fit in the plan. Her place was on these prairies, beside this man, raising their children, those children their link to forever.

"Are you ready to go?"

He helped her back into the saddle. The weariness seemed to be gone from her, but she did notice, uneasily, the light was fading from the sky.

But Evan saw it differently. "Good," he said. "Mac might have matches. I hope he'll light a fire. If he does, it will show up for a long way."

"If he lights a fire," she said, "it will mean he wants us to find him."

Twenty minutes later, the sky still holding sunset, but the earth blanketed in darkness, she heard Evan's yip of triumph, and saw the flicker of the fire in the distance.

Evan pushed his horse into a gallop, and hers followed. Holding the horn, the first stars coming out, feeling as though her heart would burst with joy and completion, she followed Evan at breakneck speed, over uncertain ground toward the future. Her future and his.

They galloped to the fire, Evan pulling his horse to a swift halt, and getting off it in one smooth move, running now. And then out of the circle of the fire she saw Mac, coming toward them, Jesse's hand firmly in his, both boys faces streaked with dirt from tears.

"Evan," Mac said, his voice quavering, "I'm sorry." He was sobbing now, rubbing his eyes with his hands. "I didn't know Jesse would follow me. I didn't know. You must have been so scared when he was gone."

Evan got down on one knee in front of Mac, and Jesse barreled by and jumped into his lap. "Daddy," he said over and over. "Daddy. Mac, I tell you my daddy would come."

Mac drew in a long, shuddering breath and stood, his head hanging, his tears splashing down into the dirt at his feet.

Kathleen managed to get off her horse and came toward them, and Evan stood and put Jesse in her arms, and then turned back to Mac.

"I was scared when both my boys were gone," Evan said. "Scared out of mind. More scared than I have ever been in my life."

"You're not scared of nothing," Mac said. "I know."

"Every man's scared of something, Mac."

"You can hit me," Mac said, still looking at his boots.

"Hit you?" Evan said. He closed the distance between them and wrapped his powerful arms around the broken little boy, pulled him into him. "I'll never hurt you, ever."

Mac's control broke. He wrapped his arms around Evan's neck and sobbed.

Evan picked him up as if he were a baby, rocked him against his chest. "You know, all my life I wanted a family to love. And when God gave me your auntie, he saw how much I needed a boy just like you, too. I should have said that to you sooner. A whole lot sooner.''

''Do you love me?'' Mac said. ''Me?''

''Yeah, you.''

''After what I just did?''

''Yeah.''

''After your truck, and letting the cows out and wrecking the garden?''

''Don't forget the bathroom window.''

Mac smiled a little crookedly through his tears. ''And the bathroom window?''

''Yeah.''

''I love my auntie Kathy more than anybody in the world. That's why I ran away. Even though I didn't show it, all I really want is for her to be happy. I could tell you made her happy, and I didn't. It made me mad and scared, too. I thought the more she loved you, the less she loved me.

''You know what made me think maybe I had it all wrong? When I turned around and saw Jesse behind me. I didn't even know how much he meant to me until I turned around and saw him way behind me. I ran back to him, and he had his stupid truck, and he was so happy I came back for him like it wasn't my stupid fault he was out here in the first place. I went to bring him home, and that's when I got really, really scared.

''Because I didn't know which way home was. I thought I'd been going in a straight line, but when I looked around everything looked the same. I tried to figure out from the sun which way to go back, but I just felt so mixed up and Jesse was so tired. He kept sitting down and crying, and telling me he wanted his daddy. After a while we sat down and I had some matches, and it made Jesse stop crying to find little twigs and pieces of grass to put on the fire. I only had one peanut butter sandwich with me, though, and I gave that to him a long time ago.''

"I hope you had some of it, too, son."

Mac shook his head, vehemently. "That's the part I'm getting to. I wanted him to have it all. I figured out I don't just like the kid, I really love him lots. And I figured out it doesn't make me love Auntie Kathy any less. It kind of makes me feel bigger than I did before. Maybe you'll laugh at me, but like I'm almost a man, now.''

"I ain't laughing," Evan said quietly.

"I guess maybe if that's the way things are, I better stand on my own two feet," Mac said.

Evan set him down.

"Me man now, too?" Jesse said hopefully.

"Oh, sure," Mac said. "But no more Mr. Stinky Pants, then. Not ever. Got it?"

"Got it," Jesse responded solemnly, and they all laughed.

Evan looked at the gathering darkness. "I think we're stuck here for the night. I don't want to risk it in the dark. Those horses are done. We'll just sit tight for now. Break out those sandwiches, Kathleen."

"Can you find your way home from here," Mac asked anxiously, "or are we going to be like the Swiss Family Robinson, only lost on the prairie?"

"Even if I couldn't find my way home," Evan said, "those horses could. You could turn them around in a hundred circles and when you were done they'd point their noses for home and go in a straight line right there.''

They sat around the campfire. The boys ate every sandwich and Evan made them both drink some coffee.

And then a strange and magical thing happened.

There beneath the stars, they became a family. The family Kathleen had pictured, the family she had dreamed of.

Laughing and telling jokes and singing. As the night got colder, Evan stripped the blankets off the horses, and they squeezed under them, and holding as tight together as they could, they went to sleep.

They woke in the morning to the sound of a helicopter beating over them.

It landed close by.

"Put the boys on it," Kathleen said. "I'll ride back with you."

"No way, Auntie Kathy. You and Jesse go. I'll ride back with Evan."

Kathleen did not miss the authority this was spoken with, like a true man, and so she climbed aboard the helicopter, a wide-eyed Jesse on her lap, and watched as her husband and her boy worked side by side to get their horses ready. Saw Evan clap Mac on the shoulder, and Mac lean into that hand for a moment, gathering strength, before he stood tall.

She watched them standing together on that seemingly endless prairie, until she could see them no more. With a sigh of contentment, she looked ahead.

Later that day, feeling exhausted and exhilarated, she welcomed the two dusty riders home, and said goodbye to the last of the search crews, her friends and neighbors.

"We're going to go now, too," Fiona Mortimer said. "Evan, we owe you an apology."

Kathleen turned to see her holding a sleeping Jesse, looking out the window.

Fiona began to speak, almost to herself. "All we wanted was for Dee to be happy. She was our only child. We gave her too much. I can see that now. We gave her too much stuff, and we gave her too much freedom, and the more we tried to fill her up the emptier she got.

"Evan, either you've changed, or I read you wrong, and I suspect it's a bit of both, but I know you and Kathleen will do a wonderful job of raising our grandson. Jesse is in good hands. We won't bother you again."

She turned from the window and put the sleeping child in Evan's arms. Blinking back tears she walked rapidly to the door.

"Fiona," Evan said. "Thank you. You know you are welcome here, anytime. And it's no bother."

Her husband cleared his throat and spoke. "We read Mac's note while you were out there, and we realized something. We have been so broken by our daughter's death that we forgot there would still be people who needed us, that we could still be of use. When we read Mac's note, we realized there were lots of kids who feel like him. Who would love grandparents just like us. We need someone to dote on. When we get back to Regina we're going to find out if there are some kids who need a granny and a grandpa to love them. Maybe that's how we can say we're sorry to Dee for loving her in all the wrong ways."

"Ron," Evan said slowly, "it seemed to me you got two kids right here that need a grandma and a grandpa to love them."

Looking pretty close to tears himself, Ron nodded, shook Evan's hand and followed his wife out the door.

"Who would have thought?" Evan murmured, watching them drive away.

"Do you ever feel as if we are in the presence of miracles?" Kathleen whispered.

"Well yes, ma'am, I do. A humble cowboy becomes a knight in shining armor. I know a miracle when I see one."

"Love is the miracle. It makes good things grow out of hard ground, it makes tears into diamonds, it makes things that are wrong right again. It gives little boys daddies like you, and a woman like me the husband of her dreams."

"You're just saying that 'cause of the way I fill out my blue jeans."

"Damn right, cowboy."

And she kissed him. It felt as fresh, as exhilarating, as intoxicating, as it had the very first time.

She knew some people were blessed that way.

They went through life as if it were a dance, as if everything were brand-new and magic, as if there were all kinds of things left to explore and to fill them with that feeling of first-time wonder.

She knew, when he returned her kiss, that she had just become one of those people.

Every single day a new opportunity to live, to laugh, to fall in love all over again.

Every single day a first time.

Forever.

Epilogue

"Auntie Kathy, Granny and Grandpa Mortimer are here!"

Kathleen wiped her hands on a tea towel, and went to the door, watching as Mac flung himself into his adopted grandmother's embrace.

"I got my report card," she could hear him saying excitedly. "Straight *A*'s. Know what that means? My dad is going to teach me how to ride bulls. Well, steers. I'm going in a rodeo this summer."

It was nearly six months now since Mac had started calling Evan Dad, and Kathleen still felt the same catch in her throat at the way he said *my dad* with such fierce pride and possessiveness.

Jesse shot out by her.

"Granny. Grandpa!"

Perfect *r*'s she noted, and felt just the faintest sadness at the passing of time, at how quickly little boys became big ones.

Jesse had said good-bye to diapers and his soother

forever after he and Mac had walked onto the prairie that day.

They came through the door, the boys and their grandparents, and Kathleen noticed the soft radiance in Fiona's face.

"How's Adopt-A-Granny going?" she asked after they had exchanged hugs.

"I still think the name is sexist," her husband groused good-naturedly behind her.

"We've had calls from all over North America asking for information. I'm going to be a guest speaker in Los Angeles next month. Me!"

"Fiona and I have sixteen grandchildren now," Ron said, "including these two." He rustled Mac's head affectionately.

"Me going to be in rodeo," Jesse crowed.

"What?" his grandparents said together.

"He's going to be a mutton buster," Mac said. "I'm helping him learn."

Kathleen laughed. "Mac bought some sheep with his 4-H money. I think we're the only farm in Saskatchewan with sheep that are now all broken to ride."

"Yeah," Mac said disgustedly, "not much buck left in them. Hey, did you notice my auntie Kathy looks different?"

She felt herself blush as the Mortimers turned their full attention to her.

"I do not!" she said.

"She's pregnant!" Mac announced officiously. "We're going to have a baby. Jess and me want a boy, but she doesn't. She'd like a girl."

"Me, too," Evan said, coming in the back door. "I want a little girl with big brown eyes and long dark hair. Hi, Fiona, Ron. Good to see you."

Kathleen watched as Ron shook his hand and Fiona hugged him. She could actually feel the love shimmering in the room.

Then he kissed her, as if he hadn't seen her for a year instead of the few hours it had been. He turned back to their guests, his arm around her waist.

"I really appreciate you coming to spend a few days with Jess and Mac. I've been promising to take Kathleen to the Cypress Hills forever. Our first anniversary just seemed like the right time."

Our first anniversary, Kathleen thought. Her thoughts went back over the year, and it seemed as if her mind was a photo album full of snapshots of moments she had once just imagined: Mac and Jesse chasing butterflies through the tall grass, their house brimming over with laughter, Evan looking at her with a tenderness that never went away.

"You're doing us the favor," Fiona said. "What do you guys want to do first?"

"The water slides in Medicine Hat," Mac said.

"I'm too old for that," Fiona said, with mock fear.

"That's what you said about tobogganing," Mac reminded her. "When me and Jesse were cold and wanted to come back in, we couldn't get you off the sled."

"These older women," Evan said solemnly, "just run a man into the ground. They're full of surprises."

Kathleen smacked him on the arm, then looked into his eyes and felt a deep welling of gratitude for all the wonderful surprises life had brought her.

"Come see my room, Grandma," Mac said, tugging on her arm. "I just repainted it."

"Thank the Lord," she said.

"All black," he said gleefully. "Even the ceiling."

''Me want black room, too,'' Jesse said.

''You have to wait until you're twelve,'' Mac told him sternly.

They had dinner together, and then Evan and Kathleen were shooed out the door, their suitcases already in the truck.

''The stars are just coming out,'' she said wistfully, after they had driven for half an hour or so.

''I suppose you want to stop?''

''Could we?''

He stopped the truck and they sat in the silence and looked at the stars. After a long time she reached into her bag and got him out a small square box.

He unwrapped it.

Inside was a belt buckle, engraved with the date and year of their anniversary.

''The silver,'' she said softly, ''was from a real suit of armor, worn by a real knight in the middle ages. The armor was damaged in a fire. It couldn't be fixed.''

''How on earth did you find something like that?'' he asked, turning the buckle over in his hands.

''The Internet.''

He laughed. ''Is the world going to leave this old cowboy behind?''

''No. The world will always need cowboys. And knights. Always.''

''Come here.''

She slid across the seat to him, into the place she loved to be most. His arms. He kissed her until they were both breathless.

''Kathleen, will we ever get to the Cypress Hills?''

She thought of the options. Kissed him again, long and hard, and said, ''I certainly hope not.''

* * * * *

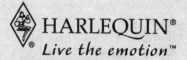

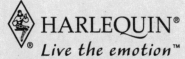

HARLEQUIN®
INTRIGUE®

BREATHTAKING ROMANTIC SUSPENSE

Shared dangers and passions lead to electrifying romance and heart-stopping suspense!

Every month, you'll meet six new heroes who are guaranteed to make your spine tingle and your pulse pound. With them you'll enter into the exciting world of Harlequin Intrigue—where your life is on the line and so is your heart!

THAT'S INTRIGUE— ROMANTIC SUSPENSE AT ITS BEST!

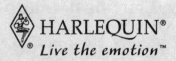

HARLEQUIN®
Live the emotion™

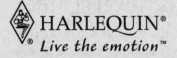

HARLEQUIN®
Presents®

The world's bestselling romance series...
The series that brings you your favorite authors,
month after month:

Helen Bianchin...Emma Darcy
Lynne Graham...Penny Jordan
Miranda Lee...Sandra Marton
Anne Mather...Carole Mortimer
Melanie Milburne...Michelle Reid

and many more talented authors!

Wealthy, powerful, gorgeous men...
Women who have feelings just like your own...
The stories you love, set in exotic, glamorous locations...

HARLEQUIN®
Presents®

Seduction and Passion Guaranteed!

HPDIR08

Harlequin® Historical
Historical Romantic Adventure!

Imagine a time of chivalrous knights and unconventional ladies, roguish rakes and impetuous heiresses, rugged cowboys and spirited frontierswomen— these rich and vivid tales will capture your imagination!

Harlequin Historical . . . they're too good to miss!

Love Inspired®

HEARTWARMING INSPIRATIONAL ROMANCE

Contemporary,
inspirational romances
with Christian characters
facing the challenges
of life and love
in today's world.

**NOW AVAILABLE IN REGULAR
AND LARGER-PRINT FORMATS.**

**Steeple
Hill®**